The Collection

Nina Leger

Translated from the French by Laura Francis

GRANTA

Granta Publications, 12 Addison Avenue, London, W11 4QR

First published in Great Britain by Granta Books, 2019

Copyright © Éditions GALLIMARD, Paris, 2017

English translation © Laura Francis 2019

Originally published in French as *Mise en Pièces* by
Éditions Gallimard, Paris, in 2017.

This book was published with the help of the
Association for the Anaïs Nin Prize, sponsored
by the Coriolis and Very.

The moral right of Nina Leger to be identified
as the author of this work and of Laura Francis to be identified as the
translator of this work has been asserted by them in accordance with
the Copyright, Designs and Patents Act 1988.

The text includes brief extracts from *Concrete Island* by J. G. Ballard
(Harper Perennial, 2008) and *Neuromancer* by William Gibson
(Gollancz, 2016).

A CIP catalogue record is available from the British Library

9 8 7 6 5 4 3 2 1

ISBN 978 1 84627 686 6
eISBN 978 1 84627 687 3

Typeset in Galliard by Patty Rennie
Printed and bound by CPI Group (UK) Ltd, Croydon, CR0 4YY

www.granta.com

The Collection

For J. D.

She slides it into her mouth.

She lets it grow heavy, take on warmth, breadth and shape, push against her palate, weigh upon her tongue.

Immobile lips, minute internal contractions: her movements have grown less frenzied.

She thinks of paper flowers that unfold when placed on water.

She moves away, and contemplates the erect penis.

Uniform sky, a dove-grey canvas stretched between the tower blocks; cars roll in an unbroken line across the horizon; at regular intervals, the varnished brown of a streetlight interrupts the alignment of the trees; cops glide by on bicycles, eyeing up the wedding boutiques: banal geometry which Jeanne matches with her steps, her breathing and her thoughts.

She walks up the boulevard.

But she changes direction, crosses, and the broken angle of her path is sharp enough to puncture the space like a nail that catches on a piece of fabric and tears along its length. The city falls apart, loses its abscissas and ordinates, creating a maelstrom of sky, trees, streetlights, bicycles, dresses. The sign on the corner of a pharmacy liquefies, flows down, mingles with the electoral posters, becomes sluggish, slips into the dead leaves, turns the tarmac over, swallows the clothes rails at Guerrisol and the iron shutters, consumes the pavement. Jeanne sinks down.

A dizzy spell, people assume, when she leans against a shop window – inhales, exhales – while the smooth coldness of the glass goes through her shirt and freezes her shoulder blades – inhales, exhales – while she closes her eyes and tilts her head backwards – inhales,

it's always when she tilts her head back.

Jeanne has drawn the curtains; the light, grown green, has filled the room like water.

Jeanne listens to the noises of the hotel – lift moving up along its cables, doors slamming, groundswell of a vacuum cleaner. It is nearly midday, the tourists have left to perform their role on the squares of Paris, their rooms are empty, the management is resuming its authority. A trolley of miniature shampoos and towels approaches, slows down, but the room is protected by the card hanging from the door handle which commands in red capitals, DO NOT DISTURB. The trolley continues its advance. Soon its creaking fades away into the carpeted distance. The lift freezes, the doors are closed for the day, the vacuum cleaner quietens. Calm descends on the room, so Jeanne concentrates on the enclosed space, on the coming and going of her hand, on that of her lips, and on that strangled breathing that filters down from above her.

She plays her tongue across the compact penis. Her

saliva follows the contours of the veins, soaks her fingers –
which she holds tight at the base of the penis, their joints
rendered smooth and white by the pressure – forges a
path between the hairs and weighs down their curls.

As though trying to gain purchase on a slippery rock,
the man puts a hand on Jeanne's shoulder. She shakes
herself free, and fastens her lips tighter. At the corner of
her field of vision, behind the man's pelvis, an aloe vera
plant carries out static contortions: bed, lamps and chairs
float, aquatic.

It's always when she tilts her head back. A dizzy spell, people assume: how could they think otherwise, seeing her back pressed against the facade, her hand stirring the air, her slightly bent knees, her head tilted back, the disorder of the body which seems ready, with one sudden fall, to rejoin the earth, a vertical plunge like a tower collapsing in on itself? A dizzy spell, people assume, unaware that she falters without feeling faint, that she knows the means to reach an end and that, always, as soon as she tilts back her head, a masculine voice – sometimes seasoned and self-assured, sometimes cracking before it is even raised – asks her, Are you OK?

She does not give his face, size, shoulders and stomach the slightest glance, for nothing in the outward appearance of a man ever foretells his penis.

She is constructing a memory palace that, as it fills with new penises, becomes intricate with corridors, annexes and outbuildings. The number of doors is always growing.

She could have taken photos and made a collection from them; she could have kept a notebook of tallies or sketches, used a spreadsheet or private diary as a back-up, she could have confessed her memories, more or less retouched, to others; she could have forgotten them. She preferred to construct a palace.

Each room of the edifice accommodates the memory of a particular penis and ensures its remembrance. Jeanne only has to cross the threshold and she rediscovers the shape, the form, the particular warmth, the density, the smell of the penis; the elasticity of the tissue and its colour when drawn tight and when slackened; the smooth or glistening appearance of the head; the network of bluish blood vessels; the shaded areas; the wrinkled fingerprint skin of the testicles; the growth pattern of the hairs.

While the rooms retain the complete memory of the penises, nothing else penetrates: the man disappears, his image consumed by Jeanne's magnified gaze.

She accumulates, but looks for nothing; she is not searching for a penis that would surpass all others and give meaning to her explorations, imposing their limit. She collects without comparison, adds without judgement, showing neither preference nor disdain. The layout of the palace ensures the democracy of the set-up, and Jeanne is not subject to sudden passions: not even for an instant will any new acquisition be favoured over the others.

Jeanne sees no need for love affairs to smooth events into a more palatable shape; she takes the sex, without deadening its shock. Her sexual geography is composed of places where bodies pass with their personalities undiscernable: shopping centres, public transport, boulevards and avenues. She avoids spaces devoted to and devised for advances, flirting and seduction: bars, nightclubs and lounges, where sex is won through subterfuge and territorial reconnaissance, where each gesture and word is directed towards an end which it would be judged vulgar and impolite to make explicit. Circumlocution, nonchalance and compliments are all essential requirements.

Where does she take the bodies that she encounters?

Not the shelter of covered porches, no entrance halls of sleeping apartment buildings, car parks, toilets, swimming pool changing rooms, telephone boxes, offices, lifts or stairwells: she rules out communal or public spaces of fantasies.

She doesn't take them back to her place, any more

than she follows them to theirs: a home would carry the imprint of the quotidian. The objects would be assimilated entirely within the narrative of a life, their assembly producing an impression of unity destined to express a past, a present, aspirations for the future; to exhibit tastes and emotional attachments; to distil a negligible, but corrosive, intimacy.

Once, in the very early days, she faltered at the entrance of a red-brick building. At that moment, a man came out. He had offered to help her; she had agreed to go up with him. The sound of the door has since stayed in her head: a lock with three bolts to unfasten, which resisted, allowed itself to be gently forced, then gave way noisily, relieved to be defeated. The apartment: beige carpet, large cupboards, a fold-up bed – which the man insisted on unfolding, but not before offering Jeanne a glass of water – two windows opening onto a park, window boxes that held no flowers, the distant sound of children below, a smell of spices, pale yellow bedlinen. These elements composed a whole that some would call a life, and others an existence, but this ensemble, whatever its name might be, evaded the collection. The man's penis was fused there. In Jeanne's memory, its colour merged with the pale yellow of the sheets and the beige of the carpet, its curve shattered by the oblique light slanting through the glass of water, its silence disturbed by the children's screams that rose up fitfully. Thus encumbered, it was unable to pass through the palace doors and instead followed the direction of ordinary memories. Today, Jeanne would not be able to describe it. Yet she remembers the glass of water, the cupboards, the park, the bare window boxes.

By excluding all other possible locations, only hotels offer the neutrality required for Jeanne's activities. She has become an expert in them; her map of Paris is dotted with addresses that she recognises instinctively. Hôtel Agate, Hôtel Prince Albert, Hôtel Prince Monceau, Hôtel Coypel, Hôtel Nord & Champagne, Hôtel Edgar Quinet, Comfort Hôtel Lamarck, Seven Hôtel, Park & Suites Prestige Paris Grande Bibliothèque, Adagio City Apart'Hotel Montrouge, Ibis Budget Paris Porte de Vanves, Mercure Paris Porte de Versailles, Hôtel Kyriad Italie Gobelins, Hôtel Kyriad Bercy Village, Hôtel Kyriad Montparnasse, Hôtel Magellan, Hôtel Fiat . . . She likes their rooms, which belong to nothing except their number, 12, 208, 5 or 43, unearthly spaces, instantly taken over and fictitiously possessed. She likes that you need only enter to give yourself up to the wildest behaviour, to the tenderest intimacy or the crudest obscenity, exposing to the anonymous bedroom walls things that you would never reveal to your most loyal confidants. She likes that you leave, that you return the key to reception and, immediately, the erasure of every trace of you begins. The sheets are washed, the towels changed, the fingerprints sponged away. The cleaning absolves the room from all affiliations, ensuring its availability and its amnesia. The image of bodies that had, only a few hours before, been close to ripping the sweat-soaked sheets, is dissolved in an emulsion of bleach, submerged and siphoned away with the dirty water. The next client will discover a perfectly new and virgin world.

Jeanne appreciates these clear-cut arrangements, the perfect repetitiveness of hotel rooms: each object there offers a serial guarantee, even the decorative innovations. If she discovers a bouquet on a bedside table, she reassures herself that, as evidence suggests, in the neighbouring room an identical bouquet is arranged in an identical vase, set down on an identical table, and that would be the case for the next room and the next and the next again, as though a single room had been designed then placed between two mirrors and infinitely replicated. Jeanne examines the multiplying blush of the flowers until they disappear into an indeterminable vanishing point. Satisfied, she double-locks the door and, hand on the bolt that confines her in the room with a stranger, reads *sotto voce* the small notice posted on the back of the door: BREAKFAST €12, TOURIST TAX 60 CENTS, ANIMAL SURCHARGE €4; SECURITY INSTRUCTIONS

IN THE EVENT OF FIRE; EVACUATION MAP; YOU
ARE HERE.

For her, these grey words are the hyper-discreet
heralds of debauchery in a standard hotel room.

There was a beginning.

That day when Jeanne's eyes focused upon the coppery glimmer of a man's flies.

Metro Line 13. A dogged accordionist struggling against the jolts of the carriage. A man, sitting opposite her, at whose crotch she stares, and who is petrified by her gaze.

The woman sitting to the man's right senses danger: her attention skims the surface of the man's face, establishes its layout and identifies the place where the landscape breaks with its ordinary topography. It is happening at the corners of his eyes. His gaze is too remote, frozen and trembling at the same time. The woman's eyes drift towards what is holding his attention: Jeanne, her eyelids lowered, eyes like searchlights, a look which lingers, which presses and sinks further into the folds of dark blue cloth and seems to draw down the teeth of the zip one by one. The man dares not bar her way. He could, quite naturally, shield himself with his hands, cross his legs, cover himself with part of his coat, but he remains motionless, divested of his rights over his own penis.

The woman squirms, would like to change seats, drag the man away with her, pretend that they are getting off at the next stop and so must stand up immediately in anticipation, for the carriage is packed and otherwise it will be impossible to make their way through to the doors. But she is transfixed like her husband, held prisoner by the system of immobilisation maintained by Jeanne's narrowed pupils.

When the train brakes at Saint-Lazare, Jeanne lets go, rises, and is gone. The couple remain sitting, drained and silent. They hold that silence, postpone the first words, suspend their criticisms – the edges of which are vague, the surfaces grey –, unable to settle upon a single adjective. Of course, they will speak, but first they make the most of having said nothing, of not knowing, for a moment, what the first intonations will be, the first investigation that will launch the spiral of badly chosen words, discordant voices, offensive questions, old resentments, tactlessness and paranoia. They know that their grievances are insoluble, since they are impossible to formulate and justify. They know that no amount of discussion will allow them to reach an agreement, that they will never share a mutual understanding of the event, but will occupy two camps, former allies who from that point on suspect the other of having played an active role in the massacre that has just decimated their troops. If a truce is concluded, there shall never be a peace treaty; an imbalance remains, a doubt, a suspicion. They used to walk together so well, but from now on they will only be able to hobble along.

Jeanne walks alongside the white-tiled walls. She follows the insignia for Line 14. Fast, precise steps, arms and shoulders swinging like a metronome, her chin raised; up to this point all is well, and the episode has been so deeply absorbed into the vaguest levels of her consciousness that she would be astonished to learn that she stared at a man's crotch for four stations. It is as though the image never touched her brain. But the process has been set in motion and, though slow, it is inexorable.

She comes out onto the underground piazza where Line 14 links up. The space widens out, natural light showers down and dissolves the electrical precision. The hard tiles melt into a smooth wall of creamy shades, the degree of reverberation alters, sounds no longer travel down the axis of corridors but liquefy into layered rumblings that disintegrate in the depths of the escalators.

That's when the image hits.

Jeanne comes apart.

She leans against the wall; inhales, exhales; the cold goes through her cotton jumper; she tilts her head back, looking for purchase, and abruptly the din shrinks to a single point: a man who stops and offers her his help.

She takes him to a hotel.

She leaves twenty minutes later, his smell on her hands, a bar of soap in her pocket. She resumes her journey where it had been interrupted, calls the doctor's surgery, tells them she will be late, apologises, thanks them for granting an extension to her appointment, confirms her imminent arrival, apologises again, hangs up – a bar of soap in her pocket, his smell on her hands.

Lulled by the alternation of tunnels and metro stations, she believes in the exceptional. From this murky moment of hormonal delirium, she will fashion a late-night anecdote for when parties empty out, when just a close-knit circle remains and when, in order to keep the group together, to stay just a moment longer sitting in the same light, people tell secrets to try to amuse the others. This anecdote, certainly, will be the perfect bargaining chip. It has the means to provoke both astonishment and curiosity. The audience will be hers; time will pass and nobody will make the slightest attempt to leave their seats. It will be up to her to provide the signal to leave. People will clamour, striving to know just a morsel more but, faced with her resoluteness, they will let her leave. Some of them will call her up the next day to continue the conversation.

Gare de Lyon – EXIT LEFT – pale neon lights. Jeanne stares at the tropical garden caged by glass walls. Dark, mordant greens; droplets of water on the branches; leaves that are upright or drooping, bushy or flat like the oars of small, agile boats; glistening stamens, grey earth. Real plants mingle with plastic facsimiles, but the brief halt at the station and the reflections in the glass make it impossible to distinguish the real from the fake.

The metro resumes, Jeanne does not realise that a new system of memory is taking form, that the anecdote will become a way of life and that her stories will remain unconfessed. Soon she is unable to summon the voice, face, size or weight of that first man. Only his penis continues to appear to her. A dark, brown penis, which grows lighter towards the mound of the head where it becomes translucent, like an electric night light in a child's bedroom.

Drowsiness, tender and shadowy folds, abandonment to torpor. Dilation, rising, elastic rigidity, too narrow in form to contain the new mass, compressed, veins protruding.

Jeanne maintains utmost concentration.

Her gestures are slow, diligent. She passes the penis between her fingers, into her mouth, presses it against her face. She examines it, occasionally putting it to her ear to listen to the blood beating, follows the curve of the head with her thumb, feels for the slit which drinks up her saliva.

She isolates the penis between her two cupped hands, excludes the body, and fixates upon the mobility of the organ that gradually fills the space. The furniture diminishes, the details blanch out. She remains alone with the penis which she has made her own. Even her own body has lost substance.

He claims to be in a hurry, but lingers and keeps on talking. As he speaks, he paces the room, turning from one object to another; he draws the curtains, opens the window, closes it again, inspects the cupboards, turns on the television, turns it off, pats a blue ceramic apple placed on the pedestal table, buzzes around the room with the excitement of a sovereign pontiff rediscovering the luxury of his summer residence.

His words and his gestures follow two perfectly autonomous channels. After having drawn, opened, closed, inspected and patted everything he can, he continues to speak, adjusting his collar, dusting down his jumper, rolling up his sleeves and rolling them down, ensuring his trousers hang correctly. Jeanne's silence makes no impression on him. He feels as though he is making conversation.

As he is checking the sole of his shoes and speaking of spring, which is decidedly late in coming, the sharp noise of a latch interrupts him and makes him turn; she has disappeared.

Surprised, he waits.

He sits on the bed, blows his nose, notices a scarf forgotten on the chair, anticipates the imminent return of the woman, waits, checks his phone, re-knots the lace of his right shoe.

When the traffic lights at the nearby intersection have turned green for the eighth time, he gets up and goes down to reception. The room has already been settled, they tell him. He leaves the hotel. After several metres, he is halted by the sensation of a foreign object gripped in his fist. He retraces his steps, leaves the scarf at reception, then disappears.

Early on, she lacked discipline: there were men she saw again, agreeing on meetings for a fortnight later, same time, same place, but forgetting their faces between each encounter. When they appeared, she rediscovered their enquiring faces at the doorway and was not struck with amazement by their handsomeness, felt no joy at meeting a longed-for gaze, no desire to take one of these faces in her hands, to gently kiss their eyelids, to trace their mouth with one finger, to come close in order to smell their breath, to bury her nose in their hair, to expose the nape of their neck and press her lips to it.

Occasionally some men fell in love; or decided to fall in love, and to claim that they had done so. They considered each meeting to be a sign of her affection, calculated the possible increase in their frequency, beseeched Jeanne not to meet them directly at the hotel but to go to a tea shop first, where they would order two hot chocolates with whipped cream and say something along the lines of 'Tell me your life story. Take my heart into your hands, break it if you want to but, first, come with me to Annecy on Friday next week, I have a chalet.'

Sometimes, in these situations, Jeanne made the mistake of reasoning with her lovers, caressing the back of their hand and telling them, in a soothing voice, with moist eyes and a cool heart, It is impossible. She might speak of a husband, cite family obligations, invent children to raise and protect from the bitter reality that weakens emotions and wears down bodies that were destined to be bound together forever. She might describe fragile, sensitive Chloé, who could not bear her parents' separation, and as for Charles, her little man, who has a conflicted relationship with his father; without her to act as an intermediary, to calm their arguments, to secretly bring him a plate of food when his father has shouted, Go to your room, and don't bother coming down for dinner, we don't want any of your insolence at the table, without her it would be a debacle, it would mean the breakdown of the filial relationship, no, truly, Annecy is impossible.

She varied the age, sex, number and name of the children – generally preferring the unremarkable (Marie, Léa, Benjamin or Matthieu), one day venturing Isolde and on another occasion, in an American mood, toying with Denver – but she grew tired of these tricks. She learned to slam doors, she became an expert in radical disappearances. The lover would leave the bathroom, body swathed in steam, and find the bedroom empty. An allegory of Stupor in a Towel, he would quickly shake himself dry, tangle himself in his clothes, dash across corridors, lifts and entrance halls at great speed and without success: no Jeanne in reception, no Jeanne at the threshold, no Jeanne in the street. There is no Jeanne at all, in fact, for the lover would believe he'd slept with Mélanie, that it was Mélanie who had squeezed her thighs so tightly around his waist that it was as though he could still feel them, it is 'Mélanie' that he had groaned when Mélanie had taken his penis in her mouth, and it is still Mélanie, Mélanie Fonville, that he searches for, breathless, in the telephone directory, on dating sites and social networks.

From now, Jeanne does not see anyone more than once, and has no further recourse to Mélanie, preferring silence in the place of a false name. She also prefers not to know the name of the man she is unzipping. If, despite everything, he speaks, if he embarks on the detail of his professional life and outlines his future prospects, she focuses her attention on the shape of his penis curving in his boxer shorts, and on the two pearly plastic buttons she will soon unfasten. The rest, all the rest, falls into forgetfulness; and Jeanne's forgetfulness is as dense as her memory is precise.

It is in hotels that Jeanne finds the necessary elements to furnish her palace. She appropriated a doormat and some candlesticks from the Hôtel Saint-Pierre, net curtains from Timhotel, bedspreads from the Hôtel du Delta and the Hôtel Cambrai, some obsolete ashtrays and two bedside lamps from the Hôtel de Nice. The palace is an exquisite cadaver of the Parisian hotel trade.

Jeanne passes through her domain in the evening, at bedtime, in the morning, upon waking; she roams around it between appointments, in the midst of loud dinners where conversations stream out without spilling a drop onto her, in the crystalline sharpness of the beauty counters in department stores, under the halogen bulbs of waiting rooms.

Sometimes, she interacts at length with a particular penis. Attentive to the fidelity of the memory, she approaches, observes, drinks in the details. Hours pass in slow meanderings and interminable pauses until she leaves the room, reluctantly, careful not to disturb the stillness of the forms.

On other visits, in the mood to make an inventory, she works her way through her estates briskly, as if to draw up a complete atlas. In her path, doors fly open and curtains flap. She turns on the overhead lights, inspects the general state of affairs, tidies any particular mess, chases out accumulated dust. She bustles around and, blind to contemplation, plays at being administrator. Nothing is working. Scrap everything, here – this is fading, there – this is turning dull, over there – something is becoming blurred. She begins fixing it up, refreshing the paint, reviving the brilliance, straightening the arrangements. She inspects her trophies in search of any defects in the fabric. If flaws affect a memorised image they cannot withstand examination, and Jeanne invariably restores the structure of the distorted penis. Sometimes, she even ventures some transformations in the layout of the palace. She plans, she considers, but then is suddenly cautious. She hesitates, her gestures are weighed down by her awareness of a risk. The efficacy of a memory palace depends on the immutability of its layout: in manipulating the order of the memories, she puts them in danger. Each room functions as guarantor for the one succeeding it. In certain intersections, a single room determines the access to a dozen others, all of which would disappear if Jeanne were unable to remember the master room. Rendered inaccessible, these rooms would survive for a time in transparency, illegible files, damaged beyond repair. They would soon be forgotten. The regular mnemonic surveys that Jeanne practises are for the purpose of avoiding such lapses in memory. Reorganisations tend to lead to forgetfulness. So Jeanne puts them away for later.

He falls asleep. Jeanne is motionless, her legs entwined with his, her ear close to his unfamiliar breathing, her face pressed against skin whose smell and texture will remain foreign to her.

Once the man is buried in sleep, she reaches a hand towards his penis, encircles it, follows the slow rhythm of its retraction, squeezes its mass, now so supple, encompasses the drowsing testicles with her fingers. She falls asleep like this, the warm, damp penis coiled in the hollow of her hand.

Silent movements wake her up; the man is disengaging himself from her strange embrace. She feigns sleep. Between her eyelids, she watches him get up, gather his clothes, pick up his watch from the bedside table and slip into the bathroom, closing the door behind him. The noises filtering through the dividing wall recreate in a minor key every movement of the unseen man. Gurglings of pipes, spurts of water, droplets hitting the ceramic tiles. When the man's body is interposed, their impact becomes muffled.

The shower curtain is pulled back in one brief movement. The sound of the water follows the curves of the body, ricocheting off its fullness, pressing into each hollow, stretching out in its folds; it climbs or falls in pitch depending on whether the hand raises or lowers the shower head. A nervous, quick plash: the man is washing his penis. Doubtless he is taking more care than usual. The water bubbles in the chalice formed of his hand, overflows and crashes down, the shock flat and clear between his two parted feet, toes clenched, nails whitened. After a few minutes the water is cut off, the plumbing gives one final swallow and falls silent. The shower head is replaced, the curtain pulled aside once more. A damp shuffling on the tiles, the rubbing of fabric and a metallic clink, a cough, intended to be discreet. The door opens and the man is there again, barefoot in a dark suit, his silhouette hazy through Jeanne's half-closed eyes. He sits down in a black armchair, pulls on his socks and laces his shoes, stands, shrugs on his coat, checks his watch, then his phone, casts a glance towards the bed, hesitates; and slips away. Because he believes he is the one sneaking out, he cushions as much as possible the noise of the door closing behind him.

Who would believe that an origin could be entirely contained within one event? No, an origin must put forward causes, factors, antecedents. It must supply, in detached pieces, the complete machinery of an existence, with which the narrative will be assembled in stages.

Yet the metro anecdote, which sees Jeanne staring, supposedly despite herself, at a man's crotch, excludes the most important aspect. It feigns naivety, confines itself to the factual and gives no reasons at all, no essential explanations that can justify such bizarre behaviour. Loosely, it produces several irregular pieces, but doesn't take the trouble to fit them together with the help of nuts and bolts, without which the whole assembly is doomed to collapse: the *whys*, and the *becauses*.

When these dissatisfactions arise, Jeanne is getting into the lift at the Hôtel de Chypre, followed by a man. The machine has barely begun to gain momentum when, breaking into the scene, a group of *whys* approach reception. The various parties lean on their elbows, frown, compulsively check their watches – I'm waiting for someone – until the appearance of their cavaliers: an elegant group of *becauses*. The hall is packed, couples form, shyness ebbs away: conversation can begin.

Meanwhile, Jeanne gets out of the lift at the fourth floor, takes the corridor to her right, swipes the card in the magnetic lock of Room 76, enters the room, approaches the window and watches, outside, a red car that passes in the street, parks in front of a green cafe from which a man in black exits. Jeanne, abandoning the scene outside, looks away and places her hand on the penis of the man accompanying her. While these minute movements fill Room 76 with their silence, the racket of *whys* and *becauses* grows in density, skims through successive strata, insinuates into each vacant space and imperiously colonises the entrance hall of the Hôtel de Chypre.

If you crossed the hall, you would hear that Jeanne is thirty-six; that after receiving her *baccalauréat* she worked for five years – first in a call centre, then as a medical secretary, that she had met a husband, her husband, at this job, the classic story: the prematurely greying ophthalmologist who presses both his hands on the back of the armchair and leans in a little too close to consult the appointment book over his secretary's shoulder; the classic story of the secretary who blushes and breathes in deeply, feeling someone else's breath scattering the strands of hair tucked behind her ear; the classic story of the first after-work drinks, to get to know one another, You've earned this, Jeanne, your work has been excellent since you started, prolonged over dinner at a small Italian place that doesn't look like much, though the *linguine alle vongole* makes it worth the detour, We make a good team, the two of us, a winning team, then another glass, Women fascinate me, their sensitivity, their connection to the world, then the hasty climb up the stairs to her studio, Believe me, Jeanne, this has never happened to me before, never, and thus the ophthalmologist and his secretary became man and wife. A *because* continues in tranquil tones that their visions of marriage tallied so perfectly that Jeanne quit her job in order to put them into practice: he was at work, she at home; he active, she contemplative; he the straight line, she the interlacing; he with affirmative speech, she with a wide-eyed stare; he with his feet on the ground, she absent-minded; he, realism, she, daydreams; he with concrete speech, she with suspended sentences that tail off, vanished in thought. Another *because*, raising its voice brusquely, interrupts this suspiciously smooth tale – There was abandonment; there was neglect, solitude and, soon, Jeanne's taste for documentaries was no longer enough to fill her days,

she registered on dating websites and began to scroll
through them – But another voice intervenes, claiming
that Jeanne is twenty-two, that her adolescence had
been devastated by bulimia, combined with an immense
emotional deficiency, a non-existent sense of self-esteem,
acne, a tortured relationship with her body, scarification
leading to a suicide attempt, which was followed by bad
company in psychiatric care, then sexuality, invested as
an outlet, the pathological sexuality of a teenager uneasy
in its own skin, a way like any other to make the unloved
body suffer, to punish it for who knows what and to
put it in danger, for if it had not been sex it would have
been drugs or God knows what – But no, that's not the
story at all! Let me tell you, as someone who knows her
well, that at the middle school she attended she was
known by everyone, from the stories of her exploits in
the toilets with prepubescent boys, a harpy, a wild girl,
they found the boys traumatised, ruined sexually, virtu-
ally castrated; it seems that even as a primary school child
there was something wrong, that people distrusted her,
so they gave her a nickname, a dreadful thing to call
a child if it were not for the fact that she so obviously
deserved it and – No, actually, her sexual awakening
came late, she had a very distant relationship with sex
for years, lost her virginity who knows when and who
knows who with, lost it out of despair no doubt, some

say as the result of a bet; others say that, tired of waiting, mocked by her friends, she *paid*, and so now she is decompensating, that much is obvious, in a sense she is avenging herself – A higher-pitched voice then states that Jeanne will be forty-three next February, never married, is in fact unmarriageable, suffered a trauma in childhood, molestation, perhaps even a rape, no one is really sure, someone from the family, they say, that would explain everything – Finally, having said all that, continues the previous voice, as she grew up she didn't resolve any of this, and the terror of middle school developed a rapacious sexuality, for she is nothing less than a bird of prey who paralyses her victims, men are reduced to the state of gerbils, unable to flee, it isn't even that she's beautiful, it's – And hysteria, have you considered hysteria? Say what you like, but hysterics are a reality, and that woman counts among them, you only need to look at her to see how – We can, of course, speak of a slight mental deficit, ventures a voice that is quickly drowned out by another – Really, she's scared, it's obvious she's scared, it's even likely that this unrestrained sexuality is just a cover to conceal another sexuality, without coming to terms with it, no doubt a homosexual tendency – Family meals have become an ordeal, even there she behaves provocatively, she titillates an uncle, she titillates another, and they are so kind that they don't dare do anything, say anything, they pretend to hear nothing when she makes remarks that should have no place at any dinner table, let alone a family table. Because she is cunning, she proceeds in allusions, it is never direct, but when you recognise her behaviour it becomes obvious, only she can always take shelter behind her false naivety – But of course, continues the first voice, imperturbable, the ophthalmologist noticed it, he obviously had mistresses, besides, they say that he could assess a patient's bottom from her inner-eye examination and that his judgement was infallible, and that he spread many legs at the end of his consultations, even some very chaste ones, but he couldn't stand the idea that his wife spread her own for other men and went crazy when he discovered the industrial scale of her infidelity, destroyed everything in his path and down she plunged, a divorce that left her penniless, an exile in the wilderness, a vale of tears, a way of the cross, a calvary, a descent into hell, once she thought she could find refuge in religion, a convenient excuse, but religion cannot redeem such flaws, it's not a miracle solution . . . She played the little saint, calmed down for a time, yet, as you would expect, the behaviour began again, worse than before, it is beyond her control.

The volume rises with excitement, the voices grow hoarse, repeat themselves, restate their arguments in ever-briefer loops, reduced to just a few words spat out, relentlessly, but none have yet said the word they all anticipate, the word around which they revolve in ever-tightening circles, the word which no one dares to let loose but which they know will appear, the word which they would all like to pronounce courageously, trembling with the risk of it, the word which suddenly rings out from the corner of the room, necks are dislocated to discover where this audacity comes from, but already the shockwave of the word has washed over and, royalty-free, it is taken up by everyone: nymphomania! There: the unknown that solves the equation. Voices erupt all around, beside themselves. nymphomaniac, Jeanne, nymphomaniac, nymphomaniac of twenty-two, thirty-six or forty-three, a redhead, brunette or blue nymphomaniac, a 34D nymphomaniac, competitive nymphomaniac, featherweight or bantamweight, a nymphomaniac for the modern era, the era of the internet and globalisation, middle-class or upper-class nymphomaniac, morphine-addict nymphomaniac, manic-nymphomaniac, genetically modified nymphomaniac, the greatest nymphomaniac in history – her mother was that way, her grandmother too, the apple doesn't fall far from the tree, and if you could go back to the Stone Age, you would no doubt find a prehistoric fornicator, a cave-wrecking Australopithecus, breaking up homes with a flint, nymphomaniac, Jeanne, or nympho, it depends: *nymphomania*, a sexuality lacking pleasure, a sad pathology; *nympho*, a fucker, a cum slut, a bitch on heat, a thirsty whore. The rhythm accelerates, explanations fragment, the adjectives destroy the grammatical constructions: crazy, vulgar, seductress, perverse, sick, the words tear each other to pieces, har–pred–dead–depr–wrec–temp–mad–bit–hys–prosti–lot–ator–beat–aved–ked–tress–woman–ch–teric–tute–slut but the lift door opens and Jeanne exits.

The crowd falls into silence, looks for an imperfect fastening, a misplaced button.

Jeanne passes.

Later, when the hallway is once again deserted, the man descends in turn, taking the stairs.

He has the bearing of a solicitor, but it is with adolescent excitement that he confides to her that he has never gone to a hotel with a woman. Never during the day, he clarifies, upon reflection.

The room has two single beds. Jeanne stretches out between them, back against the carpet; the man kneels down, one leg on each side of her hips; she takes off his jacket and shirt, unbuttons his trousers, frees his penis and masturbates it.

She gently breaks her grip, places her hand as high as possible, lets the head rest against her face, grips, extends her movement. When he comes against the curve of her cheek he freezes, stupefied, as though what just occurred had nothing to do with him.

She leaves the room, cheek reddened by the texture of the eucalyptus-scented toilet paper.

The penis was very long, perfectly tubular. The testicles, small, seemed tied tightly at the base, they accompanied the motion without ever amplifying it. No hair disturbed its streamlined slenderness. The man seemed proud of its shape.

The front window of INTIMATE SECRET is flat and glistening. It neither overhangs nor is set back from the boulevard, there is no curtain or canopy; it keeps strictly to the line of the building's facade. Laid out in the window is a theatre of dolls and mannequin torsos. Fabric moulds or veils the metallic bodies, light as helium balloons, sleek as car bodywork. The materials are iridescent, pastel-toned, diaphanous, and their contrast with the angular poses of the mannequins they adorn carries a discreet sense of unease.

INTIMATE SECRET belongs to a chain that prides itself on a clientele that is 60 per cent women and couples. With Christmas coming, the window is filled with feathers and fur. Those who pass by on the boulevard glance inside, but without turning or slowing their pace. Faces sink back into the folds of scarves, conversations follow their course. It isn't as though the shop frightens or shocks them, it's that it allows itself to be forgotten. They barely see it before it is already a memory.

When, on one dull morning, Jeanne enters the boutique on the boulevard, she discovers a sparkling universe. Reflections ignite, float, then shatter. The plastic boxes have the hard brilliance of crystal, their edges concentrating the light in sharp lines, the products that they protect disappearing in a vague, desirable shimmer. Jeanne advances, screwing up her eyes. The floor itself seems icy. Some shop assistants glide by, rustling, their smiling expressions and glossy lips recalling the alliance of vulgarity and wellness characteristic of the 1990s. They are attentive and come to the aid of customers who stagger here and there, thin birds caught in the glare of headlights. The shop assistants restore their bearings. Serenely, they take hold of the articles that the customers dare not touch and handle them with dexterity. In their hands the reflections die down, the sparkling enchantments loosen their hold and the objects appear, at last, accessible. They encourage a purchase in simple terms. They talk about the connection between quality and price, about practicality, efficiency, with technical precision. The decisive sales pitch consists of associating sex toys with wellbeing. For this, the sales assistants evoke studies. The American study on the G-spot, the Canadian study on the prostatic orgasm, the Japanese study on the nerve endings of the clitoris. For novices, they relate the study recently published in *The Lancet*, which proves

Nina Leger

that masturbation has the same relaxing effect as thirty minutes raking leaves in a zen garden. The name of the scientific journal has an effect. They have already heard about it, somewhere, on the television or the radio, an assurance of reliability – a British assurance, moreover.

This one should be reimbursed by social security, laughs a sales assistant, addressing Jeanne. In her hands, an ovoid object, peacock blue, soft-looking. With sinuous gestures, the shop assistant traces the contours of the object; accompanying the hand, the voice enters into considerations regarding flexible materials and minimalist design. She underlines the shape, which has nothing explicitly sexual about it, but resembles a pure harmony of curves and counter-curves. Liberated from realism, sex toy becomes *bel objet*. It is respectable, and can be kept in plain sight – nothing about it would mar the surface of a varnished console table.

With discreet steps, a woman joins the conversation. Head lowered, she acquiesces and smiles at appropriate moments. She fixes Jeanne with the damp eyes of a devout assistant at the baptism of a newborn. She reaches a multi-ringed hand towards the sex toy and murmurs, It is marvellous, it has never let me down.

Jeanne is no longer listening, a pink and blue pulse hammers at the back of her skull: flickering neon lights, sexual zone preserved, obscenity reclaimed.

42

VIDEO SCREENING – LOTS OF CHOICE – PEEP SHOW – BLOW-UP DOLL – SEX BOOTHS – POPPERS – CUT PRICE – FULL-FRONTAL NUDITY – DVD – GADGETS – SEXY LINGERIE – LEATHER – LATEX – X: the rue Saint-Denis, the Pigalle quarter or the Rue de la Gaîté bristle with the signs, placed high up. Not with delicate twinkling, but with screaming neon, and with fluorescent stickers on the shop windows – arrows, speech bubbles, stars, flashes and explosions – that spell out offers with the help of explicit diagrams. The entrances are barred by curtains of red, blue or black velvet.

From the central reservation in the middle of the Boulevard de Clichy, positioned under the plane trees, Jeanne observes. Most of the time, nothing happens, and the neon lights exhaust themselves in vain, illuminating faces that remain indifferent to them.

But, from time to time, someone enters – a sudden veering from a straight path, a deviation so abrupt that nothing seems to have anticipated it, their entrance into the sex shop giving the impression that they have succumbed to a sudden whim, a decision nothing could have predicted, that continues to elude forecasts.

And, from time to time, someone comes out – this specimen, thrown too abruptly into the din of the street, sways on the threshold, blinks, undecided on the attitude to adopt and not entirely certain he wants to go to where other people are waiting for him. But this period of hesitation is enough to restore to him an age, a sex, a socio-professional category, a family, friends, projects and tasks – all the things that were forgotten at the entrance of the sex shop. Regaining his contours, he slips back into the city and moves away, gradually adjusting his pace to match the rhythm of his existence.

These returns to identity always happen with hands in pockets. It is a banal gesture, which serves as an antidote to the shameful. The higher the pockets are placed – vents in a jacket, or close to the chest – the stronger the degree of denial expressed. Hands buried in the front trouser pockets look spurious, those which reach the back pockets confer an air of detachment which only works if the facial expression matches – otherwise, these are the two indicators that betray the crime; hands planted in the pockets of a long coat remain suspicious, they could be clutching onto a still-hard penis through the flannel lining.

Some women come out as well, but never alone. Most often, they are on the arm of a man who is carrying a bag, and whose face exudes a self-assurance, as well as an acute sense of ownership. Sometimes, they appear in a group, giggling and pink, drunk with the joyous delight of their transgression.

If they meet Jeanne's gaze, they nudge one another, whisper, come to a halt, crane their necks to see her better – a distant, hazy figure under the plane trees – and move away, casting uneasy glances behind them. The men never notice her. They are too preoccupied with their pockets.

Jeanne also discovers a specific category: tourists. Fresh off a coach parked not far away, the group advances with a great deal of noise and begins a meticulous, hilarious examination of the shop window. They call to one another, pull on one another's sleeves, point at incongruous words and signs. Laughter binds the group together. Their cohesion comes at the price of abandoning their sexual beings. They have left them in the coach with their bottles of water, cereal bars and any objects of value that the guide advised them not to keep on their persons. Thus lightened, they speak of sex as though talking about a ridiculous adventure that only happens to other people. Once they have exhausted the resources of the front window, they enter with small steps, in single file, backs slightly bent as they pass underneath the curtain, fearful and over-excited at the same time, as though entering a haunted house at a fairground. Some time later they exit, victorious, and they regroup on the pavement in a compact accretion of pastel puffer jackets. They have made purchases, but not for themselves: they have bought presents. Each sticks their nose and their hand into another's bag, discovers their purchases, grabs them, hauls them out, presents them to the group, feels them, turns them over, returns them with peals of laughter.

By means of this joyful search, the group verifies that its members have chosen their items derisively, and that no one has taken advantage of the opportunity to satisfy a desire that the others have silenced through a collective consciousness. The anxiety is perceptible, and the buyers whose bags are being checked laugh harder than the others, in order to prove their distance from sexual matters.

When suspicions have been quelled, the group leaves in the direction of their coach and continues their Parisian trip, their bags bulging with kinky dice and naughty bunnies, but preserved from debauchery. Next stop, Montmartre.

The man's penis has a smell that she doesn't like. It is curved, with a very red glans and green veins, vindictive, visibly clean, but its vanilla odour nauseates her. She moves it away from her face and points it towards her stomach. The man reinstates it with two shuffles of his knees. New attempt; new reinstatement; new attempt; new reinstatement, swifter still than the first two.

Of course, there is much that has not been said about Jeanne.

One could describe her wardrobe;

her technological objects (model of her mobile phone and computer, possession or non-possession of a toaster, a television, a hi-fi system, a laser or an ink-jet printer, etc.);

her trinkets (leather bags bought at the flea market, photographs, animal companions living or stuffed, holiday souvenirs);

her habits (coffee or tea in the morning, culinary tastes, Saturday hobbies, Sunday evening pastimes);

her connection to the technological objects mentioned above (frequency, duration and recipients of her telephone calls, frequency, format and recipients of her text messages, usage or non-usage of photographic equipment included or not included with her mobile phone, whether she listens to the radio or watches television (if so: which channels, and in which time bracket), her possible piracy of audiovisual products, whether she reads or plays games on her tablet, buys or sells goods online, uses social networking sites or dating apps with geolocation);

her job, the description of which would provide an opportunity to specify how successfully her working hours and earnings fit with her way of life, sanction it, and ultimately assure its credibility. The professions offering the most watertight justifications would be those allowing Jeanne to work at home, with flexible hours: perhaps a graphic artist, an illustrator of children's books, or a free-lance journalist. So she would work in a luminous apartment – white walls, south-facing, beautiful high ceilings, a view onto the zinc arrangement of Parisian rooftops, a functional yet modern layout, its decoration exhibiting the characteristic tastes of the creative class.

Yet Jeanne could also easily be a lecturer, for a lecturer works few hours, and demonstrates qualities long-proven by novels, qualities that equip them with the mystic power to give body to the most uncertain personalities. As a lecturer at a provincial university, she would regularly take the regional train, group her teaching hours into two days, spend the night in a Citadines Apart'Hotel or in a pied-à-terre lent to her by a colleague. As a lecturer at the Sorbonne, there would be a pretext for describing the hills and valleys of the Latin Quarter, cafe life, the heavy doors that open onto studious libraries, the prestigious and central figure of the professor in her lecture hall. Her apartment would, of course, be modified accordingly. It would be shadowy and wooden – oak floorboards, exposed beams, Persian carpets and antique furniture. At night, she would turn on the lights in their opaque lamp-shades. Their faint glow would cast light onto annotated books lying open, snow globes used as paperweights, pens, paper clips, a collection of tiny picture frames. The rest of the apartment would remain plunged in a darkness that would never be frightening, but cosy, and conducive to elevated thoughts. The noises from outside would be extinguished at her front door.

However, despite its multiple advantages, the professorial solution has its constraints. That is, the inevitable sexual relationship nurtured by a professor with one or many of their students, a juicy apple into which every reader of this genre wants to sink their teeth. Placed at the beginning of the story, or in the middle, the event usually marks a tipping point, launching the main character onto a slippery slope. Though the student–teacher relationship permits some titillating possibilities, it soon carries with it the cumbersome spectre of psychoanalysis – the incest complex is not the least of it. In a story that takes as its principal subject the sexual life of its heroine, the lecturer is a facile narrative device, as well as a risk of potentially catastrophic consequences.

Jeanne, therefore, will not be a lecturer. No more than she will be a graphic artist, an illustrator of children's books or a freelance journalist. She will not even be a writer.

There will be no reverse side to the set, as the hotel rooms are not a stage; no concealed wings, in which Jeanne sheds her ordinary self in favour of an extraordinary costume. We will not catch her by surprise, absorbed in the tribulations of dressing-up, cinching, moulding, revealing, toning, tapering a body held in the spotlight.

We cannot distinguish the contours of this body, nor the objects that surround it, nor the status that animates it. Is it one of those bodies that change and appear suddenly several years later in another form – filled out, or slimmed down – with a complexion, a haircut and an attitude that are not those you used to know? Or is it one of those rare types that are unchanging: elements of the child persevering in the adult, as much as the latter is already visible in an outline of the former? Is it striking, or neutral? Is it well proportioned, or does it display those irregularities which can sometimes contain the beauty of a figure – and often, its failure? Jeanne: is she beautiful, or is she sexy? Is her body loud? How does her skin absorb or reflect the light? Do her hair and eyes match in a unity of brown or do they contrast, enlivened, blonde and black, chestnut and blue, red and grey? How would you describe her gait, her bearing? Does she hide her laughter behind her hand, or stifle it in her throat? Does she sneeze quietly, or in a burst? What is the rhythm of her breathing? What is the smell of her sweat, that of her breath? Is her mouth dry, or is it moist? What is the taste of her sex?

Jeanne's face flickers with the rhythm of the neon lights. At first blue, then pink, then yellow, then blue. She presses herself so hard against the windows her thoughts condense against them – first in fine condensation, soon in slow droplets, which seep, ooze and run onto the pavement in a thick, electric pool.

She leaves.

She comes back.

The neon lights absorb the last dregs of the day and make the nights uniform: winter and summer are identical, traversed by the same pulse, clouded by the colourful exclamation marks that make the sky more opaque, blacker – an abstract plane, all stars swallowed.

Buds curl on the branches of the plane trees; then elastic green leaves unfurl, white veins stretching out, and, one day, the green ebbs, shrivels up, ochre, crackling, brown needlepoints; the leaves contract,

fall.

Finally, one afternoon in Pigalle, she enters.

Situated on a cobbled street with plant tubs, the place, answering to the inexplicably spelled name of SEX-SHOPE, presents a door which advises: Pull hard. A reassuring set-up, the place announces its rules and protects newcomers from the shame of making a faux pas, of becoming entangled in the undertow of a curtain with no way out, of a stumbling, farcical arrival onstage. So Jeanne pulls hard and the door opens; a relationship of trust is established.

Incense paper, thick carpet, various strains of world music that vie with one another, reddish lighting, deep purple display cases; heads turn, alerted by the gentle hiss of the hinges, and look away with unease; objects are placed back down, steps retreat, take shelter at the back of the shop, as the intruder advances.

Jeanne disregards the gimmicks stacked in lavish pyramids: penis-shaped pasta, candy breasts, Kama Sutra card games and apple-vanilla lubricants.

She lingers for a moment in front of the accessories: lingerie, handcuffs and fantasy costumes.

A few steps further, she reaches the area dedicated to sex toys. This time she stops, stands in front of the shelves, gauges the ideal distance from which to take in the full view. At the upper reaches of her gaze: geisha balls, medium-size dildos, rabbits, ducks. Approaching the summit, the shelves take on the appearance of an armoury. The plastic bristles with metal, and the dimensions increase: this is the domain of the extra large. After familiarising herself with the general layout of the territory, Jeanne approaches, extends a hand, tilts back her head and begins to rummage around the shelves.

The silhouettes, obscured since her entrance, have not returned. Despite the background music and the jingles that interrupt at regular intervals, the shop is suspended in perfect serenity. Jeanne is the sole point of unrest in the room. She crouches down, rises again, steps to one side, stands on her tiptoes, contorts herself to capture a distant object, each limb participating in the effort, until her head, which pitches from one side to the other, hesitates, stops, and plunges forward. The jumble of objects is so dense that each rummage risks a collapse. With her free hand, she averts any falls.

Slow, silent, the silhouettes leave the shadows. Suspicious as moray eels, they give Jeanne a wide berth. Her effervescence remains solitary and incongruous, an isolated bubbling in a leaden body of water. Several times, the door reprises its hiss: certain people prefer to leave while her back is turned. Others proceed, nonetheless, to the till. They pay in whispers and leave, after having shaken the hand of the shop assistant who apologises mutely for any inconvenience caused.

Leaving the SEX-SHOPE, Jeanne pauses, stares at the slightly-too-blue sky, slightly-too-red geraniums, the facades of the houses huddled close together against the cold. At the end of the street, the boulevard breaks the stillness of things. Windscreens and wing mirrors appear in flashes; leaves catch in the light and swirl as though locked in a snow globe. Jeanne buries her hands in the pockets of her coat and moves away, towards the metro. A white plastic bag rubs against her leg – inside, a silicone penis slipped into a purple box with a transparent window.

Air bubbles form. Images rise and burst on the surface.

The man who, at around 5 p.m. in winter, at the moment when she closes her eyes and feels his glans at the entrance to her sex, tells her, Don't fake it.

The one who, in his urgency, tears a button off her shirt, gathers it up, keeps it clasped in his hand while he penetrates her, before carefully placing it in his wallet.

A velvety rubbing against the insides of her thighs: the man didn't want to remove his trousers, and contents himself with sliding his penis through the unzipped opening of his flies.

The one who, positioned by the window of the Ibis Paris Berthier Porte de Clichy, points out the constellations that he sees appear in the sky one by one, and those that he cannot see but must, nonetheless, be there. Cassiopeia, Orion, Perseus . . . His voice trembles as he steals calculated glances towards the bed, without understanding that despite its stellar character, the charm of his litany is equivalent to that of a recitation of multiplication tables.

That other one, who places a hand over her mouth to muffle the cries she has no intention of emitting.

One, with rounded back, who sits masturbating at the edge of the bed.

Another, who calls his wife from underneath the covers, whispering to her that the meeting is dragging on: that she should arrange whatever she fancies for dinner that evening.

The trace of a white vest that shows through a starched shirt, also white.

An armpit, hairs pearled with sweat where the electric light plays in sparkles. Jeanne stares at the flickering of this delicate garland, until one particularly vigorous movement launches one droplet onto her cheek and another into the corner of her eye. The man comes and asks her if she is crying.

The ossified curls of slicked back hair.

Narrow hips, receding below the waist like a mermaid's tail.

A nipple, pale and pink, childish fold of flesh with no areola.

The sudden depth of a brown iris, into which the light plunges.

Lips pulled back over two rows of teeth, as dense and tightly packed as those of a zipper. Incisors, canines, molars, each identically sized.

Jeanne is not bothered by the arrival of these images, whether they are old or recent. There is no hidden logic in their choreography and they are barely liberated before their drastic reduction is carried out. All surplus visions dissolve and the palace rediscovers its calm. Only the penises remain, avidly contemplated, and in the sharply angled corridors, Jeanne's steps once again ring out in perfect solitude.

She confided in her friends. After the initial surprise, the encouraging 'tell me's and the ardent expressions burning to clarify each detail, none could resist the temptation to diagnose: voices go back over the facts in minute detail, tut as they utter pertinent articles of law, swell, digress, drumroll as they accelerate towards a verdict – the pleasure of judgement.

They all attached gestures to their words.

The female friends tugged on their earlobes, ran their hands through their hair, shook their head when they listened and when they spoke, their slender hands with long, varnished nails improvised to underline each remark, a spiralling set of gestures that alluded both to rhetorical science and to the ritual of seduction.

The male friends leaned their forearms down on the table, the edges of their hands swept the tablecloth with the regularity of a windscreen wiper, as though to assemble Jeanne's sins into two lateral embankments.

When the time came to pass sentence, all gestures

ceased. Rigour is called for, nothing could interfere with the honesty of the speech that chose to express itself in domestic terms, for it is obvious that Jeanne needs to settle down, put her life in order, make a fresh start, a clean sweep, to stop trawling through such filth and behaving like a slut. The guillotine blade of judgement fell, and its sharp sound conveyed how confident Jeanne's friends were when it came to distinguishing the clean from the dirty, order from disorder, them from her. They drew a straight line between causal relations and explanatory outlines. They uncovered primary causes. They brought to light patterns that were bound to have escaped her notice, lacking as she does the necessary distance to understand the workings of her own intimate narrative.

Leaving these meetings, Jeanne had her arms full of a thousand and one personal records, while her friends had a brighter colour than when they arrived. They had lived more intensely for a few minutes, uncovered secrets, exercised their psychological fibre, helped a woman in distress.

The childhood friend advised her to sign up to a dating website for serious relationships; the friend who is married to a sexologist gave her the contact details of some specialists and recommended she join a Sex Addicts Anonymous self-help group; the friend of everyone offered to put her up for a few days in her country house; the friend who is an enthusiast for fatherhood told her it was essential that she become a parent; the friend met by chance considered it absolutely crucial that they see one another again and take some time to speak calmly about it; the friend of a friend asked her why she thought it necessary to talk to him about it.

They all perked up having given their opinion, but more than anything, they buzzed with the opportunity to tell a transgressive story – Darling, do you know what Jeanne told me today? – between the lentils and the yoghurt at the dinner table; the dreadful tale – You won't tell anyone, of course? – will be able to reunite the most devitalised of couples and offer them a moment of communion. Each will recognise the image of the urges they have bravely conquered in order to become the normal individuals they are now. Under the kitchen lights, the man and woman will congratulate one another on battles fought and won. They will rediscover the vivacity of their first conversations. Once dinner is eaten, the table cleared and the washing-up stacked on the draining board, they will return to their own occupations. He will make sure she cannot hear him tapping away on his mobile phone, she will decide to do some tidying up in her sent messages and inbox. From time to time, a 'Do you love me?' will reduce the depth of the silence. That will be the moment to exchange a look, a smile, a gesture with which each ascertains the blissful ignorance of the other.

Jeanne chooses to keep quiet about her secrets, and lies. She performs the role they provide for her. She conforms, in order to better disappear.

She lies to the childhood friend, to the friend who married a sexologist, to the friend of everyone, to the friend who is an enthusiast for fatherhood, to the friend of a friend. She would have liked to lie to the friend met by chance, but goes straight to her voicemail.

Over the course of some months, she develops her script. Firstly, she puts an end to it; then she settles down; looks for someone, finds someone, moves in with someone. The friends declare themselves delighted. A slight disappointment is, however, perceptible: the loss, so soon, of such a juicy tale, cannot occur entirely without regret. To this imaginary man, Jeanne gives a first name, a job and a personality. She details their adorable arguments, mentions their plans for the future – oh yes, they're looking ahead; yes, they've planned a big trip for this summer – and voila, now she is engaged. Certain friends grow suspicious, others are thrilled. She blushes when her secrecy is brought up, promises to organise introductions that never happen. When she announces that the marriage has taken place in the strictest privacy, her audience has dwindled to almost none and the few who remain don't even pretend to believe her.

The room solidifies in a block of silence. The light has disappeared. The contours only reappear after a long time infused in the half-light. In contrast, the sheet is so white it dazzles.

The heavy, shrunken presence slowly detaches itself from the void. A cavernous body, veined with lichen, a stagnant body, enmeshed within its own mass, a life form from early times.

Somewhere in the room, the man's eyes come to the surface – two motionless stones that fix upon the nape of Jeanne's neck.

Vrrrrrrrrrr-click-silence, the noises of the street gradually return – a car horn, the sigh of a bus, some calls; a ray of sunlight passes across her mouth, she stirs her leg and her knee encounters a cold body part; she props herself up on her elbows; mattress stripped bare and sheet at low tide; washed up here and there are technicolour crustaceans, fuchsia pink or fluorescent green.

Numerous visits to the SEX-SHOPE have encouraged Jeanne to abandon the frontiers of male anatomy to discover penises more extra-terrestrial in form. These penises now occupy half of the shelves. Their layout is reminiscent of the display cabinets at archaeology museums visited during excessively hot summers. Over there, bellies of amphorae, necks of alabaster vases, chalice craters or the spurs of triremes. Here, the essential multi-rhythm rabbit vibrator with rotating head; the ergonomic dildo with silicone studs; the geisha balls with ribbed surface and flexible extraction cord; the Lust Fingers Tickler; the inflatable, extendible latex dildo with a squeeze pump that allows unlimited adjustment of the diameter; the vibrating egg; the I Rub My Duckie massager; the playfully designed vibrating banana; the powerful and silent wild rabbit vibrator, the protruding points of its muzzle and ears designed to offer a more intense pleasure; the realistic dildo equipped with a robust suction pad that adheres to all flat surfaces in the house; the mini-vibrator Compact Pro which comes with four interchangeable end pieces, tight studs, spaced-out studs, nodules and a smooth, rounded tip; the most sophisticated oral sex simulator on the market for unprecedented sensations; the realistic vibrator, curved towards the G-spot, triple stimulation for triple pleasure; the vibrating silicone ring with a silver button, allowing for the delicious massage of desired zones; the vibrating dildo mounted on an inflatable cushion assuring flexibility and stability; the vibrating penetrative underwear with elastic straps guaranteeing sumptuous clitoral sensations as well as delicious vaginal stimulation; the Big Max realistic dildo, supple and smooth, with testicles, sleekness combined with flexibility for an unparalleled intensity; to the Fuck My Hard Cock masturbator in Fanta Flesh, black, velvety, veined skin, with architectural testicles, a massive relic hovering above the crush of objects and covering their disarray with its shadow.

*

Initially, she had been an abstinent collector, touching only with her eyes, and when she decided to make use of her possessions, she didn't know how to work them. She searched for a user manual but found only hygiene instructions. She sunk her fingernail into the silicone and watched the crescent moon imprint fade as the material regained its shape, sniffed at the odour of plastic, assembled the detached pieces, inserted the AA and AAA batteries, examined the transparencies, tested the vibrations by squeezing each toy in her palm and grew accustomed to the buzzings, intermittently smooth and convulsive, distinguished the low-pitched bass rhythms from the shriller ones which got out of breath while gathering speed, she compared diameter and length, discovered functions that lit up, exhausted her wrist with manic button-pressing, all this at a distance, without daring to bring the objects close to her sex, without looking to get the slightest pleasure from them, only a preliminary dexterity.

One day, she went out to buy a water-based lubricant.

She spent a long time in front of her wardrobe, composing a meticulous bouquet of sex toys.

She pulled off the bed sheets, threw herself onto the bed, switched on the objects that demanded to be brought to life, removed the cap of the lubricant and began a slow exploration.

The tissue retracted when it came into contact with a substance that was not skin, under the weight of surfaces that were too cold, too impassive. The nerves were irritated by these unnatural, inorganic throbbings. She drew the object away, gathered it to her slowly, before pressing it harder against her. The blood flowed, swelled the tissue and gently the object grew warm, seemed to sweeten, soften and melt into her climax.

He is afraid.

When she tilted her head back, he approached, placed his shopping bag at his feet, asked if he could help her and perhaps, insidiously, he knew what to expect, maybe he even hoped for it, without really daring to believe it. But now that everything has become real, now that he is following this woman, he is afraid.

She doesn't sway her hips, doesn't turn around to throw him burning glances, applies none of the conventions of eroticism.

The shopping bag which he is holding at arm's length seems to grow heavier and heavier. With each step, he feels as though he is sinking into the ground. Yet he follows her; doesn't dare run away, transfixed with fear, but also with the hope of seeing the continuation of the erotic sequence promised by this opening shot: a woman faints before his eyes, then takes him to a hotel on the boulevard, where she reserves a double room.

He imagines what may follow: they are alone in the

lift, the background music washing over them, a burning tongue trails around his ear, a strap falls, admiring hands explore his torso, breasts brush against him, buttocks arch for him to fully appreciate their curve, the woman suddenly presses a button, stopping the lift's ascent, and dives for his zip . . .

Dreaming, he gets hard. By the time the lift arrives, he has successfully persuaded himself that his fantasy had the value of a prediction and rushes in, impatient for the doors to close and for the film to begin. The woman presses 5, and the floors flicker by on a glass screen. First floor, the woman does not approach him, does not touch him, does not speak to him, appears deep in thought, her arms hanging loosely by her sides – no tongue, no strap; second floor, she raises her eyes to the screen; third floor, she hasn't moved – no groping hands, no surging breasts; fourth floor, she throws him a glance, brief as a toe dipped in cold water – no buttocks, nor curve; fifth floor, she approaches the doors which will soon open, which indeed open, and she walks out.

He picks up his bag, grown heavier still than it had been on the ground floor. The woman is far down the corridor, her steps are fast, her body moves forward without hesitation or awkwardness. He drags himself out of the lift.

*

When Jeanne inserts the key into the lock, she hears a voice whisper from behind her shoulder, I have to go, I'm sorry, goodbye.

She turns. The young man moves with swift steps towards the emergency staircase. A slight limp tilts him to the right and the bag he is holding scrapes against the floor. Jeanne looks at his shaven nape, the elephantine folds of skin at his elbows, his black T-shirt stamped in yellow capitals with the inscription SEX INSTRUCTOR.

The vaulted corridors span a river whose currents have frozen. Hoods, bags carried aloft, and some children perched on shoulders float on the surface. The flood has solidified into a press of motionless bodies. Impossible to reach the platform, impossible to attempt a retreat towards the exit. The only viable action that remains practicable is breathing, but the air is so humid and warm it feels more like drinking.

Synthetic voices panic through invisible loudspeakers – an unwell passenger, traffic completely halted in both directions, understanding, as soon as possible, inconvenience caused, thanks.

Jeanne's nose and cheek are crushed against a yellow anorak. She studies in close detail the reticular structure of the fabric and the distribution of several drops of rain, survivors of a morning shower. One by one, they tumble down. Jeanne licks the smallest and the roundest. Against her tongue, the anorak feels like a pumice stone. She presses her forehead against it. The yellow grows warm, liquefies, flows, tepid and thick as an egg yolk that has been pierced. Jeanne drowns in it without anyone noticing her, a dead weight carried by the solid density of the crowd. The liquid engulfs her, goes up her nose and into her mouth when she tries to scream. She sinks, and the noises disappear. She makes out voices announcing the imminent resumption of service, then everything dies away. She stops resisting, sinks into the vapid warmth, reaches the depths. The space has grown soft, time has disappeared until, suddenly, she hits a cold, sharp-edged crystal carpet. The seconds tick once again. Her foot kicks against the bottom. Pain spurts out, knee, thigh, back, neck; she writhes and flails, frenetic, feels as though she is sinking deeper still, but the murky density lightens, yellow, opaque, then translucent, contours take shape, misshapen ghosts, she advances; when she emerges, she is on the platform, the light is white and the voices have fallen silent. The anorak dives into a carriage, she flings herself forward in pursuit, the doors close behind him and she remains on the platform where the bodies now circulate without touching one another. The yellow smear of the anorak disappears as the train accelerates.

She leaves the Hôtel Voltaire. She has borrowed a bed from the hotel, mounted on tall feet of white wood; wide, single-glazed windows at least 1.5 metres high; as well as a ceiling light.

This will furnish the next bedroom.

As for the penis whose memory she carries, she arranges it in a verdant bedroom where a curtain filters the daylight. She does not know from which hotel the wall hanging was stolen, but the image of the black penis, semi-erect, drawing towards repose, falls into place like a dream.

Madam, excuse me. Excuse me, Madam. The voice's refrain alternates the structure of the sentence and the placement of emphasis in order to increase its chances of, finally, being heard.

But Madam is akin to a high-relief sculpture installed on the metro seat: she doesn't move.

Someone grabs her shoulder, squeezes it and sinks in their nails. With a jolt, Jeanne emerges from her reverie and discovers two alarmed eyes, and a mouth which splutters, Excuse me, Madam, could you please close your bag? The request contrasts so sharply with the urgency of the tone that Jeanne asks for her to repeat it, and the repetition bursts out, urgently, in a whisper icier than a scream, Close your bag.

For the bag perched on Jeanne's knees has slumped to one side with the movement of the train, revealing its contents to all eyes and, notably, to the round and shining eyes of a fat, curious baby which the angry woman is holding tight against her.

The baby contorts himself, reaches out his arms, twists his mouth, spreads his fingers wide, concentrates so hard he forgets to breathe, throws his full weight forward in order to escape the maternal embrace. He wants to get at the toy poking out of the lady's bag.

The mother repeats, Your bag. The words seep out from between clenched teeth, the sentence dwindles to nothing.

The plaything is an enormous squeeze-bulb dildo.

The child has already begun screaming, Mine!, hurling himself towards the object. Heads turn. The scene is noticed. Looks are exchanged, chins jerk; fingers point towards the drama.

Jeanne closes the bag. The child rages, all snot and dribble. He bawls, IIIIIIIIIIT'S MIIIIIIIIIINE!, and pummels his mother's thighs. She waves a stringy, off-white comfort blanket under his nose in an attempt to compensate for his unsatisfied desires. The blanket is trampled underfoot.

Jeanne ventures to touch the child. Her gesture dies in the space that separates her from the small, angry body: the mother has confiscated the child, squeezing him so tightly that his sobs are stifled in a squeak. Eyes aflame, she whispers, Don't touch him!

From that point, her existence composes itself as an empty set – without names, without titles and without definitions. If a discourse winds itself around her, she welcomes it, she lets it wander in search of handholds and points of connection, she encourages it in its misunderstanding. When the discourse lowers its guard, certain of having captured her without a fight, she tears into it. Strand by strand, shred by shred. In the light of day, the discourse has disappeared, some remnants lying at Jeanne's feet.

She has a notebook in which she had planned to keep a diary. Large format, small squares, spiral bound, lemon-yellow detachable pages, an infringement of all the aesthetic principles of a private diary. Unable to find the first words to fashion a narrative about herself, she has let it transform into a notebook of expenses and other things, abandoned terrain where weeds grow. There she notes her spending, chores and shopping lists, some dates. In moments of boredom, she covers the margins with geometric drawings – interlocking voids and solids, careful striations, straight lines and curves of little significance. Occasionally, a hotel address or a room number floats on a page. On the back cover, on the rough cardboard, a vast and complicated map is drawn, the limits of which are uncertain. Used pages have been torn out. The irregular scraps clinging to the spiral binding form sheer coastlines with overlapping contours.

At one time, she looked for her alter ego in novels and sometimes thought she had found her there. She trawled through books that staged the sexual life of female characters. She read enthusiastic reviews recommending these texts, presenting them like so many maps of the Dark Continent, results of previously unpublished explorations that have, finally, brought long-closeted mysteries of female desire and pleasure to light. They promised far more than a novel: they promised the truth.

Jeanne plunged herself into these books. In each new text, she hoped to find what the previous had lacked. But the same pattern was invariably deployed. At the beginning the heroines were bold and immoral; the first pages blazed, the lines throbbed with subversion. Then, this heartbeat diminished, became a minuscule pulse which dwindled little by little, until vital functions shut down completely; halfway through, the heroines had been irrevocably transformed into psychological composites devised for the purposes of explication and the novel, which had appeared free and wild, preferred to frolic in an enclosure of highly limited significations where sex could be nothing other than a symptom, the sign of a void that needed filling, of an anguish to be appeased, of a slowly healing wound. The taste for sex itself was not a strength, but the consequence of extreme weakness. Incapable of existing as accountable subjects, the heroines lived only to be the objects of male desire. They relinquished all force and will to him, dreamt only of being possessed, reduced, debased, and the portrait was perfect only if their eyes were blue, their hair blonde and fine, their complexion pale, their bodies fragile. There were lots of coffees and cigarettes, and alcohol consumed in one gulp, *pains au chocolat* nibbled and immediately discarded, dark circles under the eyes, tangled hair, lips bitten hard enough to draw blood, confrontations in the mirror, sleeping pills, tears shed in public toilets, scenes in clubs or bars that culminated in these beautiful cold fish, drunk and sprawling, ending up under the opportunistic sheets of a man whose penis was never described, because it was a symbol, an authority to which the weak woman who had believed herself to be strong surrendered herself, a phallus, not a cock. And often, there was redemption. This appeared in the shape of a man – psychoanalyst, friend, husband or lover – who had the bravery to go in search of the soul – extraordinary, despite being broken – when others merely took pleasure in the body.

Now Jeanne reads science fiction, stories of reinforced concrete, of petrified forests, of chrome cockpits speeding along the rollercoaster of autoroute interchanges, of computers the size of cathedrals, of neon lights lashing against graphite skies and magnetic fields rendered hysteretic by asteroid showers. In these novels, interior motives are reduced to silence, annihilated in the collapse of ancient worlds that crushes all futures with it, and Jeanne likes that better.

He said that he was called Victor. It seemed to fill him with hope, as though his name would be a password, as if pronouncing it would open the doors onto an inextinguishable conversation. It also appeared to move him, as though in saying his name he was entrusting his life.

For some people, Victor must be a centre, one of the focal points around which a life is structured. For others, more numerous, he is located in an intermediary zone: close but autonomous, he belongs to an organisation without determining it. For others again, he circles in the periphery, his trajectory is random, his name disappears in the profusion of acquaintances, extends further and further away into chance encounters and reminiscences. For Jeanne, he does not even approach this distant orbit. While she slides his erect penis between her thighs, the signal Victor emits is so distant that she does not detect it.

But on certain unpredictable days, the functioning system jams.

Is this due to the light, to a certain internal meteorology, to the layout of the places or to the particular disposition of the men that she meets?

On these days, bodies speak even in the heaviest of silences. Each movement communicates moods, questions, impatience, frustration, feelings of a life wasted, of infinite expectations, of disappointments never overcome, of age, of habits, of tastes, of desires. She is distracted by a wrinkle, by a smell she notices, by an awkward look, by a sigh or the inhalation that precedes a swallowed word. She feels battered by the assaults of existences that are crying out to be recognised. On these days, a Victor could wring her heart.

The danger is there.

She makes the decision to stop completely, considers it all finished and her recklessness sealed off. She is seized with retrospective terror. She deserts the palace and falls back on her wardrobe and on the sex toys that save her from the risks of face-to-face encounters. She does not have to appropriate these penises, they are already hers. She does not have to isolate them from a quantity of other information, they offer her calm abstraction. She does not have to fear their speech, they have no desire to get to know her. And she does not have to memorise them, for they are always available.

So she decides to seek pleasure only in the mingling of her flesh and numerous silicones. She accustoms herself to other mass relationships, to penises that no longer face her, but pursue her body. Her wrist becomes the locus and the end of all sensation. Her orgasms occur with brusque jolts, they are never final and could repeat without end if an act of reason – or merely remembering the time – does not prompt her to extricate herself from them.

Her gaze does not come up against a stomach, it is not pushed against a pillow by the thrusting of hips. It travels as far as the bedroom wall, sometimes passes through the slightly open doorway and escapes into the adjacent room, where nothing has disturbed the flat geometry. The stillness of the parquet floor irritates her sensations. Her eyes search for a point to fix upon, and she often comes while staring at a plug switch, the foot of a blue armchair or a ball of fluff, unseen until that point, and which she decides, in full throes, must be dealt with immediately. She removes the toy set to maximum vibrate and, her sex swollen, seizes the broom and quickly sweeps the floor until a trickle of lubricant, sliding down the length of her thigh, then her calf, sends her hurrying to the shower.

During these exploits, the only things moving are mechanical and regular; all movements are vibratory: when a battery dies, an artificial penis freezes inside her. Often, the sounds betray her, the smoothness of a material squeaks on her tongue, the rigidity of another clashes against her teeth, an object falls from the bed with a dull thud. And, above all, the sex toy does not grow engorged, no veins protrude from it, it doesn't ejaculate in intense waves or brief bursts, and it has no odour other than that of plastic.

The only living body in an unmade bed, Jeanne finds herself suddenly ridiculous. Some time later, she reopens the doors of the palace and, soon, crosses a street, stumbles, takes refuge against the shop windows, her expression distressed, her breathing ragged; someone offers to help, and it is with renewed attention that she discovers the unknown sex. The warmth of the skin almost makes her laugh with joy. But, dully, she worries about these panics, which seem to be occurring with greater frequency. She suspects that fear is gaining ground.

She takes the penis into her mouth before it is erect. She feels the folds of skin dissolve in the warmth of her saliva. She has placed one hand on the inside of his thigh and the other in the blond hairs. The penis is a soft water-colour pink with a tracing of delicate red veins. The penis swells at a perpendicular angle as though the testicles – skin pulled taut, ready to tear – acted as counterweights and prevented it from pointing fully upwards.

The man takes Jeanne's head between his hands, applies a metronome movement, presses it against his pelvis then draws it away. The room rhythmically disappears and appears. With each offbeat, the shepherdesses, motorcars and swallows on the wallpaper peel off and flutter around the man's hips.

She floats in the dense perfume of her neighbour; reflections dance on the windows of the carriage, the moon is blurred and misty; the metro flies above the lines of red and yellow headlights; a new page turned.

Jeanne misses her station.

'Given the peculiar topography of the island, its mantle of deep grass and coarse shrubbery, and the collection of ruined vehicles, there was no certainty that he would ever be noticed at all.'

She stays in the train until its terminus and continues reading.

Like Jeanne's palace, the SEX-SHOPE displays a concerted sexual architecture. But, rather than a safeguard, it sets up a burial: at the back of the shop, a flight of steps plunges down – BOOTHS, says an arrowed sign. Masturbatory practice is thus dispatched and confined underground, hidden from the respectable eyes of clients on the upper level who purchase to take away rather than consuming on the premises, who can thereby ignore, or pretend to ignore, what happens below, with the reckless abandon of those who prefer to dance on active volcanoes.

Belatedly, Jeanne probes these oubliettes.

With silent steps, she goes down the stairs. The room is still, the doors shut. A line of red lights indicates which cubicles are occupied. She stops on the penultimate step, one foot hanging in space, one hand pressed against the metal handrail. Some actress's screams slide under the doors. She pricks up her ears, strains to hear further than the isolation of the cubicles permits, to discern the sound of hands setting upon penises and drawing back fabric that has become inhibiting. She would like to experience the extreme concentration of the person whose arousal is reaching fever pitch, who must at all costs contain it, to last for just a bit longer, must not gorge himself or yield too quickly to the images, must hold on for a few more shots; or, in contrast, the rage of the person who squeezes tighter and goes faster, leaning one hand on the partition wall facing him, tensed as though ready to burst through the screen, sink into the recalcitrant surface and take possession of the treasure denied to him, a moan in his throat, eyebrows furrowed so his eyes nearly disappear, mouth twisted, the vein in his forehead knotted, exhausted by combat, unable to give up.

But nothing filters through. No rubbing, no sliding, no groan. Only the screams of actresses. Jeanne has placed her foot on the floor. Apart from a few stickers applied randomly, the doors are rigorously identical, simple as those of a gym changing room.

So, Jeanne imagines.

She pictures the succession of upright penises, unaware of one another – heads haloed in televisual blue, hands rubbing, beats and offbeats, brisk movements, accelerations. She pictures the way the hands grip the penises – using the little finger or tucking it away; the thumb directly against the penis, or overlapping the index or middle fingernail; sliding the hand vertically or with light twists; pulling on the ridge, or tugging upwards to nearly encase the head; modulating the pressure or – the sound of a cubicle unbolting, Jeanne dashes back up the stairs. The person who comes out sees nothing of her, apart from the sped-up image of a pair of feet fleeing towards the upper level.

She launches herself in the direction of the shelves and absorbs herself in contemplation of a vibrating vulva simulator. Catching her breath, she listens to the steps of the man who is climbing slowly, disconcerted by the race without pursuit that has just rattled the staircase. He emerges – silhouette grey and clouded in the corner of Jeanne's field of vision. She stays still, does not turn around, but senses the gazes of other shoppers turned towards her, all designating her. She doesn't blush, and feigns regular breathing. The silhouette passes behind her, reappears at the other corner of her field of vision and exits the SEX-SHOPE.

Back at her place, all curtains drawn, Jeanne works out her plan of action; she assesses the available space between the armchair and the table, considers positioning a cushion to give a firmer foundation, seeks the perfect incline of the screen and the perfect degree of luminosity, disables her internet browser history.

So she opens up her bedroom to dozens of floating bodies, interchangeable and partial – truncated necks, heads out of shot – designed solely for sexual practice; the bodies judder when the connection drops, they are frozen in full movement while the loading wheel spins on itself at the centre of the image, interrupted by advertisements, concealed by flashing banners and deleted when clicking 'back' interrupts the video and reloads the homepage.

Red leatherette bench seat; a fire crackles in the dry-stone fireplace; the girl walks into the shot, too-tight bra, frilly underwear. She displays her bottom, rolls down the elastic of her underwear, pulls them back up on her hips, pushes her bottom out, then looks at the camera, lowers her underwear. 'You like that, huh?' she says. Parting her thighs, she exposes some more of the whiteness of the flames at the back of the shot.

Another scene takes place at a doctor's surgery, there is a skeleton to the left of the desk, almond-green walls, and Post-it notes where a caduceus winds. To the right of the video, VIAGRA FOR 50 CENTS, LEVITRA FOR €1.50. The patient confesses: she experiences pain while she makes love. The doctor is attentive: he will have to examine her and, in order to examine carefully, he gets his cock out. Soon, he disposes of his glasses. Then the stethoscope bouncing against his stomach. But he keeps his gloves on throughout the duration of the act. At 10 min 56 sec, a pair of breasts enters the room, followed by a nurse. The scene continues.

Salmon-coloured underwear on a camouflage-print sofa. Brick wall. Fingernails painted in three different shades of blue, she jiggles her ass. A man masturbates, watching her. Under the rectangle of the video, a girl sucks her thumb in a horizontal banner: $1 TRY NOW. The man gets up, close-up on his erect penis, then on the two slender hands that manoeuvre the girl's bottom, preparing for penetration. Several back and forths, cries and grunts, the penis withdraws, brief jets of sperm, fingers caress the penis to expel some thick drops and wipe them on the bottom of the girl, whose face has disappeared out of shot a long time ago.

There are five or six of them in a fake marble jacuzzi. Asses float, a few cocks emerge before plunging back underwater. A man with red hair sits on the edge, his profile to the camera, and is sucked off by a brunette, whose enormous breasts he weighs in his hands without batting an eyelid. A blond man sodomises a second brunette, who pulls from the water the buttocks of the first brunette, between which she plunges her tongue.

Jeanne presses pause, gets up, rummages in her wardrobe, changes sex toy, and settles in again.

One winter day, she diverts from her method: she does not lead, but follows; she does not invite, she accepts.

The thirteenth arrondissement, Place Louis-Armstrong, end of the afternoon. The sky ripples, roots throb beneath the tarmac, a draughtboard of lit-up windows is displayed on the facades and Jeanne observes the alternation of lights – bitter white fluorescent striplight; low-wattage wall light; the blue breathing of a television; overhead light casting an antique, lethargic yellow.

A man approaches. He is elegant – a generic kind of elegance. He proposes – euphemises, skirts. Jeanne is surprised. She is unaware of the rules of this game, as she ordinarily plays an entirely different version. However, she assents. With an assured, encircling gesture, the man indicates the hotel with aubergine drapes that mutely awaits them on the other side of the road. After you, he murmurs, indicating to her to cross.

The Hôtel Villa Lutèce displays four stars and promises 'the charm of the Latin Quarter'.

The man makes a reservation. The reception is as gloomy and purplish-blue as the drapes. A thick carpet is slashed with arabesques; a fake fire flickers weakly in the fireplace; mustard armchairs squeeze together; a cheap touch of exoticism, a twin-trunked yucca shoots out its naked spokes. Cosy music cloaks these disparate elements.

The bellboy accompanies them as far as Room 114. Once again, the man yields the way to Jeanne and, in single file, all three go down a long network of corridors papered in red. As they progress, the redness seems to intensify, and the air itself becomes tinged with embers.

At last the door to 114 is opened, the bellboy steps aside, and the red gives way to a geometric world, fractured black and white – walls, tiles, curtains, carpet and bed-covers, equally divided in alternating patterns.

The room is a duplex. On the lower level, two bathrooms, one with a shower, the other with a bath and toilet. For her comfort, the man suggests to Jeanne that she make a brief stopover here. Discreet, he will wait on the upper level.

The water runs and Jeanne undresses.

She sits on the edge of the bath, feet on the fluffy bath mat, her back turned to the filling bath. Anxiety has settled in between her ribs. Her palms smooth her knees in small circular movements. She would like to leave, to stop the game.

When a credible amount of time has passed, she turns off the water, gets up, moistens the back of her neck, her armpits and sex, slips on a robe monogrammed with the letters HVL, leaves the room, switches off the light with a trailing hand, climbs the staircase, walking only on the black squares, and hears, before even seeing it, the dull tapping with which the man designates a place on the bed where he is stretched out.

In boxer shorts, a reclining Roman Emperor, he invites, reassures, smiles.

He lays Jeanne down on the mattress, rises, looks at her from above and plays with the fastening of her robe.

Each movement indicates a routine refined in advance. He eroticises the moment, his aim is to stir up desire, frustrate it, in order to kindle it further.

He rolls his shoulders – nature tamed by culture, virility bridled by decorum, domesticated for the occasion: we are not beasts, but we used to be.

With one movement – schlak – he unknots the belt, and with another – flap, flap – he strips the woman bare, throwing both sections of the robe back on either side of the sprawling body.

He pushes his head between Jeanne's legs and begins to lick her vulva. She tenses. The tongue sinks in. A trickle of saliva runs between her buttocks. She squeezes her legs together, attempts to expel the head. The man rejects the movement, presses both his hands on her inner thighs and flattens them against the mattress. She panics, but can say nothing.

When the face emerges, satisfied and damp, two amphibian arms pull him back up to Jeanne's level. He positions himself. Before the first thrust of his pelvis, he caresses Jeanne's face, comments on her legs, her mouth, smiles indulgently, kisses her, then penetrates her slowly, using his right hand to insert his penis. When he considers the degree of penetration sufficient, he removes his hand, breathes in, pushes his hips forwards, sighs, tilts his face towards the ceiling and progressively intensifies the movement, then speeds up, slides one knee up to rest against the mattress, winds an arm around Jeanne's hips and lifts her towards him. He bites his lower lip and looks at the ceiling.

Jeanne stares at the man's reflection in a wall mirror. Her own body is camouflaged by the mass of combined sheets and covers. She sees only her face and, above, the masculine body that is stirring the bedclothes.

The man gets dressed. He had expected better.

He is certain of having behaved perfectly: he paid for the room, paid with his own money, hadn't given a second thought to the expense and afterwards had demonstrated the greatest respect towards the lady, the lady who he'd gone down on – without even asking that she go down on him. He had demonstrated such fervour and had been met with a refrigerator – an iced-over refrigerator – into whose guts he had ejaculated only by some miracle, or perhaps his own expertise. But could he still consider it an orgasm, with the bitter aftertaste of time and money wasted? He forbids himself to respond to that question but does not think about it any less.

As he is a gentleman, he hides his disappointment in bonhomie and places his honour in his affability. While he gets dressed, he asks Jeanne some stock questions, intended to facilitate his exit, to weave a continuum between sex and life, to assure the woman, before the goodbye and the forgetting, that she was not merely an object of consumption, but a veritable subject of interest. He hopes that she is not about to ask him for his number. He will claim an imminent move abroad – the United States or Singapore – for professional reasons.

She hadn't seen his penis. She hadn't touched it. She hadn't smelt it and could scarcely have described its shape. She knows nothing of the nuances of its skin, the outline of its glans.

Despite the skilfully staged virile epiphany, the penis remained a blind spot. The man had done all he could to conceal it. Jeanne's sex marked its first hiding place, then in order to get dressed he had turned around, slipping on his boxer shorts as though stashing away an object in a protective case, an object of value, needless to say, for he had not hidden his penis because he was ashamed of it, he had hidden it because it was too precious for the occasion.

He left, invoking a dinner on the other side of town, clarified that he'd paid for the room, that she shouldn't worry herself about a thing, that he was happy to have made her acquaintance. Before the door had quite closed he said, See you soon.

Jeanne stays in the room. She turns on the television.

A small group of men and women form a circle on a wooden terrace.

The women are in long dresses, cut low at the back, hair falling to their hips. Perched on high heels, they skip about, wave their hands, push back flying strands of hair, laugh and embrace one another.

The men – suit jackets over patterned T-shirts, jeans and bright trainers – demonstrate a more subdued excitement: gently swaying, occasionally rubbing their hands together.

When two new arrivals pass through an opaque glass door, they move as a pack to go and welcome them, issuing greetings – the boys brief and dynamic, the girls elongating the 'e's or the 'o's, almost singing.

Suddenly, a low voice broadcast through loud-speakers interrupts these embraces and asks the participants to go into the house. Docile, men and women start moving – the women spreading their arms to balance their precarious seagull steps.

Camera change, the low-angle shot of a living room, the individuals split up onto various sofas, armchairs and poufs. Jeanne finds she cannot leave the bed. Between her thighs, the man's saliva dries and pulls on her skin.

Two knocks at the door. Before Jeanne has time for anything at all, she hears the key turning and the door opens on the lower level. She puts on the robe, descends a few steps.

A young woman is there, pearl-grey uniform, hand towels gathered in her arms. Noticing Jeanne, she stops, blushes, then hastens with apologies, checks the room number, consults a folded piece of paper in the pocket of her overalls, hesitates, explains that she found 114 registered in her service duties, though she had said how bizarre it seemed that a room had only been reserved for a few hours and that it would already be free, she said that there must have been a mistake, but they'd confirmed to her that the room had already been vacated, so she is embarrassed, even though it isn't her fault, she will go and let them know that the lady is still there and that the room is occupied. As she speaks, she places the towels on the floor as though she is laying down weapons, without taking her eyes off Jeanne and taking care to make no sudden movements. Jeanne, from the stairs, and in a voice that she does not recognise, interrupts her: no, there is no mistake, or rather, the mistake is her own, she should have already left a long time ago, following her husband who, she adds, has already left the room and is waiting for her for dinner on the other side of town, on the stroke of 8 o'clock, but she fell asleep, due to jet lag no doubt – they have just come back from Singapore and are catching a plane tomorrow, to the United States – she fell asleep and she has made herself late, moreover, it is lucky that the young woman has woken her: she just needs the time to get dressed and then she'll clear out.

Jeanne lies without intending to do so and without understanding why. She blushes even more than the young woman in uniform.

The young woman slips out, disappears into the corridor, where she sets about busily reorganising her cleaning trolley while she waits. She hums to indicate her absorption in the task but Jeanne, back upstairs, senses her presence like that of a stranger on the metro or in a cafe, who listens to your conversation while pretending to look elsewhere. The young woman isn't fooled, Jeanne is certain of it.

Out of habit, she believed that a DO NOT DISTURB had been hung from the door handle and had rendered her invulnerable. She pictured herself hiding away, imagined protective double locks and conceived of the room as a hermetically sealed vase that could not be threatened by any invasion from the outside.

There she is, dressed, shoes on, ready to leave. In their house under surveillance, the contestants engage in a pillow fight.

Located next to the Hôtel Lutèce is a tropical pet shop, a 'reptile specialist'.

Jeanne presses her hand against a terrarium.

A bearded dragon is resting on a branch, its body drier and more gnarled than the wood.

The reptile costs €175 including VAT; Jeanne could purchase it if she wanted to possess a life. She would feed it on the crickets that are chirping on a neighbouring shelf; she would monitor the temperature and hygrometry of the terrarium; she would put in a large 100 watt heating lamp – appropriate sun for a miniature universe – and would regularly remove the animal's accumulated excretions. From time to time, she would bring the beast new twigs and stones and modify the general arrangement of the terrarium in order to guarantee a constant impression of novelty.

The shop is about to close.

A white snake patiently reorganises its coils.

A psychedelic grass snake is hidden behind a small poster that states:

LIVE ANIMALS ARE HALF PRICE.

She walks from shop display to shop display, following windows rather than streets. She progresses haltingly, lingering for a long time in front of some signs, as though a secret pilgrimage ordered her to stand there in silent contemplation. A stationery shop, a pharmacy, a Carrefour supermarket, a shoe shop, a coffee roaster's.

She goes into a toy shop, stops in front of the dolls. PINK FASHIONISTA BARBIE, rippling hair, legs crossed, shimmering with rhinestone and feathers; SCHOOL-TEACHER BARBIE, one arm pedagogically raised to the blackboard, sympathetic and encouraging smile, blue skirt flared at the knees; MODERN PRINCESS BARBIE, arms at her sides, head tilted to the right, fuchsia frothy dress compressed by the soft plastic of the box . . . all assigned to their roles by the translucent fastenings that shackle their wrists, their waist and their feet.

Sometimes she dreams of determinisms, of imposed plans of action, of identities that you shrug on like a ball gown and golden shoes.

'He knew that sunlight was pumped in with a Lado-Acheson system whose two-millimetre armature ran the length of the spindle, that they generated a rotating library of sky effects around it, that if the sky were turned off, he'd stare up past the armature of light to the curves of lakes, rooftops of casinos, other streets . . . But it made no sense to his body.' She closes her book. Haloed by the sun, the metro slides between icy apartment blocks. The carriage is as quiet as an aerial reading room. Here and there, women are sitting – necks tilted at broken angles – absorbed in large hardcover books. There is no noise other than that of the rails and the pages. Jeanne falls asleep.

The orange death throes crackle on the walls of the bedroom. Stretched out on her stomach, she watches the last flickers of the streetlight and thinks about the penis belonging to the man who left a few minutes before – a pale, wrinkled, crumpled penis that, once erect, revealed a multitude of beauty spots.

She crosses the interior threshold of the palace and looks for a place to put it. She moves around slowly, takes pleasure in pausing, explores infrequently visited rooms, ventures to the ends of corridors. She opens a door that has stayed closed for a long time. The room is blue and bare. In the middle is a square wooden table. A bar of soap, pink with brown cracks, dribbles on the enamel of the sink; a bath mat patterned with fish rots gently; the skeleton of a plant is sunk in a terracotta pot.

Jeanne looks at the soap, the plant, the wall. The recollection takes shape. She believes she is mistaken. She closes the door, takes a few paces along the corridor, opens it once again in a swift movement, as though to catch the secret activity of the furnishings. Nothing has moved, and the memory does not change. It traces the outline of a penis that is, in every way, identical to the one belonging to the man who left a few minutes ago. The size, the touch and the mass are similar; the placement of the beauty spots superimposes perfectly, to the extent that the twin penises are one and the same.

Jeanne had already met this man, she had already undressed him, had already taken his penis in her hand, had already felt its pressure against her stomach. She had already been astonished by the whiteness of its skin, curled in on itself in successive folds, and by that extension revealing a secret constellation.

Was it in the same neighbourhood, was it in the hotel next door? The Hôtel de l'Aviation, or else the Hôtel Selva?

While the last glimmers of sodium die at the foot of the bed, Jeanne goes over her lapse in memory, tries to conjure up a place, a face, a voice or a stature. But the void is complete, all is correctly dissolved. The streetlight buzzes, at its last breath. If she were to meet this man again, nothing would disrupt the continuity of her indifference. He would appear to her in the guise of a perfect stranger, his profile wouldn't stand out in the melee of a crowd, his presence would remain without outlines. The streetlight goes out. And if she leaned against a shop window, and he came to her without any ostentatious sign of recognition, she would ask him to follow her with the certainty of meeting him for the first time.

She decides to force the rules of the palace which, ordinarily, only accept unique images. She duplicates the bare room, the wooden table, the sink, the bath mat, the plant. The framework of the palace creaks and grates, the memory rumbles. To pacify the edifice, Jeanne differentiates the twin room: she repaints the blue walls in white thickened with pink, yellow and pale ochre, and there she stores the duplicated penis, which nearly disappears against this background, tinted an identical shade to its skin. The only distinguishing feature is the geometry of scattered marks that seem to be projected on the walls.

Carmine red, powder pink, black and white, a few touches of Chartres blue, soft green, beige . . . in each vignette appears an iconic, easily recognisable scene. Their arrangement makes up a large stained-glass window of virtual sex.

In a sports hall, a woman in fishnet stockings hangs on to the pulley of a weights machine, arches her back, parts her legs. Positioned under her bottom, a man in a short-sleeved khaki shirt licks her, his tongue pointed in an isosceles triangle.

On a sofa, a woman masturbates one man while a second watches, collapsed in an armchair, a bouquet of plastic flowers abandoned at his feet.

A banner appears: THESE MAMAS FUCK FOR FREE. NO CREDIT CARD. NO SIGN-UPS. NO SCAMS.

A paunchy man with brown hair fingers an Asian woman through her white underwear.

Three blow-up mattresses heaped in the limited shade of a palm tree, two striped deckchairs and, in a pink mini-skirt and skin-tight BEVERLY HILLS BABE T-shirt, a housekeeper cleans the pool. The gardener – naked under his waxed apron patterned with Provençal motifs – appears and takes her from behind on the left deck-chair. The husband arrives, lies in wait, observes, makes an attempt at anger but, overwhelmed with arousal, sits down on the right deckchair and masturbates while watching the scene.

BETTER THAN WHORES! SEND A MESSAGE AND ASK FOR A FUCK. NO MESSING. REAL PROFILES. SEE PHOTOS.

A bourgeois living room, comfortable and over-decorated, American style. A mother is sitting next to her daughter's boyfriend. She speaks to him, she is concerned. Her dress is minuscule, her breasts spill out over the top, her suspender belt protrudes from below. In the roiling of the sofa, she comes closer to the boyfriend. He is a virgin, and she's going to show him how to satisfy her daughter, for who better than a mother . . . ? She strokes his cock through his trousers while parting her legs, and starts to masturbate facing the camera. The young man watches, his face seized by convulsions. Then he takes off his trousers and underwear. The mother kneels on the sofa and begins to suck him. The daughter enters the room, freezes on the threshold, stunned. The boy gets up, approaches her, lifts her onto the living room table, takes off her underwear, fingers her sex a little, then takes her. The mother approaches, comments and advises. Every now and then, the boy touches the mother's breasts, distinctly bigger and heavier than those of the young girl.

SICK OF JERKING YOURSELF OFF? FIND A BABE TO PULL NEAR WHERE YOU LIVE AND SCREW HER TONIGHT. CREDIT CARD NOT NECESSARY.

In a fitted kitchen, a skinny teenage boy presents his cock for a thirty-something woman, who seems to be playing the role of housemaid, to suck. She goes into raptures over the size of the thing – which bears no relation to the physique of the teenager – undoes her black blouse and takes the cock between her enormous breasts. The adolescent opens his mouth and pulls in his chin, stunned.

Jeanne has spent hours in front of the screen. She thought she could exhaust the available resources – come to an end, like when finishing a book, certain of having tied up each thread of the story, of having staunched every sentence and every word, sometimes sad, but always relieved, because the end must come, that was the way things were. But new videos are constantly being uploaded to the site, their proliferation exceeds Jeanne's viewing capacity.

Without stopping, cocks remote-control bodies in the direction of holes. Perpetually hard, frozen in their masterful tension – industrious, unwavering, smooth, pink, glistening, shaved at the base, fully swollen, the glans rubicund, the shaft veined, with neither rest nor leisure they penetrate, probe, pull out, reposition, return, push, persist.

Jeanne watches and the details blur; colours wear away; sounds lose their meaning; the volume flattens; movements fragment; bodies exist no more; lines and shapes arranged on a plane; strict assemblies of cylinders and holes; theorem on the function of concavity. The machinery trips over the repetitions but continues to run, a headless chicken that limps desperately from the swimming pool to the kitchen, from the doctor's office to the sofa, from the jacuzzi to the sports hall – a man in fishnet stockings is slumped on a beige sofa, a young woman performs oral sex on him, but her husband appears, in a short-sleeved khaki shirt, and takes her from behind at the same time as an Asian man cleans his pool, while a woman in white underwear enters the scene and starts to masturbate him in a fitted kitchen while the mother plays the housemaid and the daughter enters and opens her mouth wide in a sports hall where an adolescent – the joints give way; the links implode in mid-air; shapes and colours disappear, swallowed up by a single mass, pink and soft; a white noise climbs, insinuates itself into the soundtrack and drinks up in great gulps the noises, the space, the contours.

Snow engulfs the screen.

The estimated delay of the 6:13 regional train to Paris is around five minutes. Jeanne taps her heel on the platform. We don't know why she is going back to Paris, we didn't know that she had left. A family event could explain her presence here, a big reunion, dozens of relatives gathered at an aunt's place on the outskirts of Évreux. Sleeping arrangements would have been organised for the various parties and, while festivities were due to go on over a lunch, Jeanne would have dug in her heels, decided to take the first train and so found herself plunged into this early-morning night where the cold muffles each sound until, suddenly: laughter.

There are only two of them, but they're worth fifteen for decibels, two girls who are walking along the platform nudging each other with their elbows and hips, two girls who double up, bend and hunch over, seized by convulsions too violent for their chests to contain.

Three boys, up till now dissolved in the darkness and silence, raise their heads and mutter as they watch them approach, minor agitation immediately detected by the control tower of the gigglers, who feign ignorance but nimbly shed their childishness and disguise themselves as women. The dynamic of the laughter is reversed, it had bent them forwards, but now it arches their backs, tilts back their heads and shakes their hair; it is no longer chaotic, but has become a roulade, an appeal, a fine, iridescent cord that soars up, clings to the electric cables and, from there, hurls itself into the sky, would fly to the moon and higher still, but ricochets off the cockpit of a passing long-haul plane, lights blinking at the tips of its wings; the tiny vibration disturbs a passenger who is afraid of flying and who – desperate to forge a link, however tenuous, with the conveyor belt of the globe unspooling through the window – attempts to catch the laugh, but it is already plummeting back towards the Earth, towards the town, towards the station, towards the platform, and hits one of the boys between his shoulder blades. Cut to the quick, the aspiring male straightens up, consults the other two and, as one, the group shifts, triangle of tensed shoulders, hands in pockets, hood up for one, eyes down for all three.

Satisfied, the girls size up the wildlife their laughter has snared. Swaggering, the boys progress towards the gazelles they must now encircle. Each group considers itself the predator, and each congratulates itself upon seeing its prey so close and reading in its eyes all the signs of surrender.

Yet the moment the groups join together, and the first words are exchanged, the imaginary carnivore buckles. The 'Hey, all right?' punctures the savage chase; laughter fades; self-consciousness creeps in; the erotic charge drains at its touch; the newly adjoined bodies no longer lust after each other; the dead weight of the real falls between them. The girls' bodies subside once again towards the pretext of childhood, the boys look at their feet, or into the distance, chewing on their lower lip. To fill the silence, they sniff dryly or clear their throats. Their shoulder blades tense, fall and reveal a certain softness in the curve of their shoulders, which had seemed square. Their pectorals disappear in the cotton folds of their T-shirts. They avoid eye contact.

They turn grey, rejoining, in the nocturnal monochrome, the scattered adults who observe the scene from a distance, conscious that those amongst them who venture too close will be singled out by these youths, made aggressive by so much excitement, and instantly become their target.

A newly arrived figure, less careful, or simply inattentive, walks past, close to the five adolescents, grazes them with his briefcase. The victim is perfect: the boys launch an attack while the girls immediately laugh their heads off, plunging into laughter as though leaping from a balcony. The shadow flees. The energy subsides again, goes out.

Two luminous cones in the darkness; movement on the platform – bags are grasped; straps adjusted; a few steps forward; clattering rails; quick procession of windows; slowing down; the image of sleeping faces behind the windows grows sharper; final stop; doors open; some descend, the majority get on. The train's halt has situated the boys and the girls equidistant between two doors. Tacitly, the boys head towards the right while the girls choose the left.

Jeanne follows the two girls and sits down opposite them. The fleeting sexual tension leaves their bodies tired and upset. Bloody dickheads, mumbles one of them, unlacing her trainers.

Now they are slumped, hoodies zipped to the chin, one's head on the other's knees, the other's head against the first's flank, cheek squashed against the hoodie zipper, mouth soft, while the saliva of sleep shines at the corners. Jeanne watches their bodies jostle until they reach Paris. Now and then an eye opens, knees move closer together, saliva runs in trails and darkens the blue of the hoodie, hair is flicked away by a hand, some movements reconfigure the architectonics of the heap.

The bodies wake up when the terminus is announced,

shift back and forth. The procession of buildings slows, the train dives under the immense glass roof. The bodies unfold, wrap themselves up and drag their weight towards the exit, shoulders slumped, the weight of adolescence on their backs.

The air is fresh, sonorous. On the steps of the train carriage, with untidy fringes and half-closed eyes, they remember in a flash their suitors from the platform. What if? But the early morning is long gone, so they lower their faces to remain incognito and head towards the RER station.

A missed encounter – the boys have left, the girls have dawdled – Jeanne releases these dull animals.

The last rays adorn the penis with unexpected lustre. It is placed on the kitchen table and Jeanne, settled on a plastic chair, stares at it in silence. The skin is ochre, heavy, exaggeratedly lined, the pink glans pointing upwards is a perfect copy of the rubber gloves that lie at the very back of the shot. The texture is matt, floury.

Jeanne comes closer, spits into her hand and, with one flat movement, coats the penis with saliva. The sun responds with a flash, a glittering blade runs across the penis to the bulge of the perfectly symmetrical testicles which serve as its pedestal.

The saliva evaporates, the sun disappears, evening falls and the penis melts into the twilight until it is just an outline, a shadow puppet out of place in this theatre of saucepans and drying tea towels.

He buttons up his flies with an air of satisfaction.

He prepares to speak. He remained silent the entire time he was naked, but now, dressed, he wishes to make his voice resound.

Jeanne leans with all her weight on the last scraps of silence, attempts a pleading look; he understands the message and ignores it.

With a precise voice, he lines up questions as if moving chess pieces. Jeanne does not respond to any of them, he accepts he must play by himself. He introduces himself, submits a short biography and goes into a description of his occupation. The windows are open, a bus halts at the lights and its panting drowns out the words he has uttered, but Jeanne understands them. She does not react. The man seems disappointed. He puts on his jacket, adjusts it with a shrug of his shoulders and, from his inside pocket, pulls out a business card which he holds out to Jeanne. When she doesn't take it, he places it on the bed.

The card is elegant, printed on laid paper, similar to

one an ophthalmologist husband would have possessed. He wouldn't have given it to his patients, of course, he would have reserved it for colleagues, distributing it generously at each of the annual conferences of the French Society of Ophthalmology, even succeeding – during the Retina International World Conference in Hamburg – in sliding it into the reticent hand of a Japanese specialist in optical neuropathy.

The man leaves the room. Jeanne remains sitting on the bed, then gets up and, from the window, watches him walk away with short strides. His erect penis had the smooth gravity of an ogive. Lustrous glans. Black, tightly coiled hairs buzz to the tops of his thighs.

Jeanne gets dressed, forgets to look at herself in the mirror, abandons the card, leaves the room, descends the stairs, goes to return the key and, there, changes her mind. Forgot my scarf, she whispers to the receptionist, who nods her assent, eyes riveted to the television screen where a tense 100-metre butterfly is splashing along. She goes back up, crosses the corridor once more, turns the key, advances just one step into the room, extends her body and her arm, seizes the paper rectangle floating on the mattress, puts it away in her purse, goes back down the stairs, places two banknotes on the counter and leaves the hotel just as a sharkish man scales the highest step of a very small podium.

The next day, she catches the metro at 15:00, the time of day for those with nowhere to be. The train is empty. She would like a packed metro, when the mass of bodies weighs down the machine and threatens to overpower the force of mechanical traction, when heads, arms and chests obstruct the field of vision, conceal the framework of metal and glass, compress the space to the extent that even the air can barely make a pathway through and the pallid light is reflected back neon, unable to flood the carriage as it does at that morbid hour of the afternoon, when it relentlessly carves out the slightest detail of the deserted decor – the letters of a truncated sonnet posted by the RATP as part of the permanent 'Poetry on the metro' initiative, the blue-white-red signage of the I SPEAK ENGLISH, WALL STREET ENGLISH advert and the outline of the seat folded up beneath – then liquefies in the grey linoleum displays.

It's an old metro with carriages, an MF67 model, the likes of which barely exist any more on Line 5, or on any other line. MF67: Métro Fer, Iron Metro, invitation to tender 1967, iron rolling stock, single-engine bogies, pneumatic suspension and regenerative braking, this would all have been explained to Jeanne if she had been accompanied by a husband who was a trade union official for the RATP. The MF67 is now replaced by the MF01, the husband would have continued, while Jeanne's attention would have wandered. The MF01 – invitation to tender 2001 – metro is one piece, a body with vestibules stretching and bending along the tracks, in contrast to the rigidity of the MF67 carriages which, in segmenting the rails at broken angles, deprives the traveller of the sublime, gentle feeling of their curvature. Jeanne dozes, the husband shuts up – she has never shared his passions.

At 15:40, her soul crushed by the light, Jeanne doesn't want to watch people engaging in sexual activity, doesn't want to see tightly squeezed flesh, cum glistening at the corners of lips and too-moist tongues. At 15:40, she doesn't want to hear a woman's moans, a man's short breaths and buttocks slapping against a tensed pelvis. Doesn't want to smell the sweat, the desire, the scent of sex. But the metro brakes, and the window inexorably frames ÉGLISE DE PANTIN in white letters on a marine background. Jeanne gets off, stumbles; a can bounces across the platform, falls and crashes into the ballast with a muffled sound; she would like to hear an omen in this sound. She takes the escalator, imagines that once she has reached the top she will be saved by a breath of cool wind, regain possession of her body and spirit, be caught up in the dynamic tracking shot of the street and walk between the buildings, heart swollen with the future. But the escalator runs gently to the end of its course. The air has the same taste as the light of the metro. Rolled into a tube in Jeanne's hand, the business card.

To get there, you need to turn left several times and right several times, cross an intersection, pass under a bridge, walk alongside hedges, skim walls, pass in front of the Armed Forces Commissariat, ignore Pouchard Tubes, ponder the meaning of life as you pass Evolia 93 and, finally, notice a girl leaning against a huge door. In a baby-pink tracksuit, she smokes a Vogue; French manicure, ponytail, platform trainers and myopic glasses, she's a porno actress. Jeanne recognises her, and quivers to see her body existing in space and living in a non-sexual way, that is to say, dressed, pensive, with a vague gaze and pale face. This strangeness makes her turn tail.

She walks, buses sigh, dogs bark at other dogs, telephones ring, shop windows struck by the sun momentarily become plates of molten metal, queues form in front of boulangeries, engines labour to start, the lights turn orange, men crouch down after their dogs, plastic bag in hand, children scream in front of buildings with wide-open doors, glasses fill and empty on cafe terraces, cigarettes burn, mopeds overtake taxis, high heels disembowel cigarette butts, pedestrians cross at red lights, iron shutters are raised and folded away, shouting voices hail or apprehend, scaffolding does headstands against the facades, gutters become clogged, pigeons dither, consignments, deliveries, pallets piled high, waiting times displayed on the screen in bus shelters, indicators slow down certain routes, helicopters, sirens, the white trails from aeroplanes, men settle themselves on benches and wait, taxis overtake bicycles, door codes validate secret combinations, shopping bags are held at arm's length, empty bags dance in the wind, bustling crowds form and then dissipate, clouds pass, days, nights.

This time, she hasn't brought the business card with her. The metro rushes into the tunnels and swallows the cryptic graffiti tags – ALVIN – ID-FIX – ROLEKUNZ2. The passenger facing her frowns, reading the *Realist Manifesto*.

After Saint-Marcel, the metro goes above ground. Model MF01, the daylight pours right down to the end of the train and falls at Jeanne's feet. Cars look smaller, pedestrians are flown over. The metro pulls up at the edge of the river – Gare d'Austerlitz – then pulls away again, gloriously crossing the Seine, twists and plunges down. The darkness swallows the train as greedily as the daylight had done, then a jolt brings it back up to ground level and freezes it in half-light – Quai de la Rapée – before the black tunnel swallows it again. After that, the darkness is constant.

Église de Pantin, escalator, intersection, bridge, hedges, walls, Commissariat, Pouchard Tubes, Evolia and the same girl, same place, mouth-to-mouth with an e-cigarette, exhaling a vanilla vapour.

The door against which she is leaning is a square metal block forcibly inserted into the brick, a mass that no hand could shift. But installed in the lower part is the rectangle of a normally sized door which the ponytailed girl opens with a push of her shoulder. Jeanne watches for the sudden invasion of daylight into the interior, the shower of light that will carve out the contours, extract shapes and colours from the darkness in which they are hiding. But the laws of radiance reverse and, in place of light flooding the studio, shadow is extracted from it, collapses into the street, snuffs out the sun and spreads out in sentinel along the fronts of the houses, as though two fingers had plucked up the world and nimbly turned it inside out.

Jeanne leans down, gathers up a white flower dropped at her feet. It's a tissue, rolled into a ball, lost on the concrete slab. When she straightens up again, she makes out the deserted surroundings, the abandoned machines, the coils of cable, the fake partition walls, the furnishings. She is in the studio, right in the middle of the space, but feels as though she has yet to cross the threshold.

She recognises the different rooms. These now exist in an interlinking fashion. A bathroom opens onto the doctor's surgery, the right side of which changes into a living room rug-sofa-fireplace, behind which oozes the aquatic light of a jacuzzi adjoining a perfunctory sports hall; which overlooks a pink bedroom. Jeanne circles, slaloms between these contradictions, imagines the corporal equivalent of this space: a fist articulated to a thigh, the extremity of which changes into a stomach that finishes in a double knee, at the end of which three fingers and a neck are appended.

Voices appear with lights, they speak to Jeanne, they extend handshakes, bring forward chairs; shooting will start soon, she is welcome to stay and watch, the girls are nearly ready, last make-up touches and then they'll return to the set. The man who gave her his card is pleased that she is there. He settles into a canvas chair, his name embroidered on the back – in every possible way, he asserts his status as director. He claps his hands and, as his outfit is missing a megaphone, cups them around his mouth to order everyone to come back on set. He calls several female names, all ending in 'a', and yells louder so his voice can be heard in the changing rooms.

Leaving the studio, she went straight back to Église de Pantin, sat down in a metro carriage and acted as though she had seen nothing, as though she had just left an inconsequential meeting. She pretended there were no residual images, that the passage from the screen to the flesh hadn't remotely altered the stakes of the spectacle. She tried to read, but kept stumbling at the bottom of page 263 of her book, 'And then, his face pink with the pleasure of cocaine and meperidine, he swung the glass hard into her left lens implant, smashing vision into blood and light.'

She didn't know how to make sense of these words, imagining them to have been directed at her. She left the book on the seat and began changing. At Jaurès, firstly, at Père Lachaise again, then at République. She took the metro in a zigzag, until losing her way at Châtelet, where she decides that she needs to see daylight. She follows the ultramarine signs, trails exit no. 7, veers towards no. 11, but lets herself finally be sucked up by the no. 2, Porte Lescot Forum des Halles.

The moving walkways expel her to the surface, in front of a sandstone head, enormous and pensive – pale sculpture at the foot of a gloomy church. She turns away and reaches the shops on the Rue de Rivoli.

She slaloms between overstuffed bags and bottled-water sellers, steps on a few feet and suddenly, as she feels a toe roll under her shoe and, as the woman in sandals next to her gives a perfunctory scream, order disintegrates. The location is no longer determinate, there are only collisions, landslides, chasms, she tries to make her way through to the nearest window display – to press her back against the cold of the glass, inhale, exhale, wait for the voice, penises in her hands, movements, smells, she knows the scenario, but something goes off course, she inhales, exhales, raises her head, no voice condenses the turmoil, the street disappears, the signs, the bags and the bottled-water sellers are suddenly invisible, while on a screen cast into the sky a pair of figures appear in 16:9 aspect ratio, a redhead and a brunette locked in relentless doggy-style. The bodies roll, gigantic, dark, loud; the enormous thrusting of hips makes the pavement shake – but that could be the passage of the metro under the epidermis of tarmac – the screams fill the space – but that could be the helicoidal call of an ambulance – the mass darkens the sky – but no doubt that's the crest of buildings swallowing the fading rays of light – the cock sinks in, thick, moist, grotesque, the brunette grasps the testicles slapping against the sky, she looks at the camera, and it is at Jeanne that she stares when she screams, in her filthy voice – 'Watch me come!' and she drums her feet, releases the testicles, grabs hold of the redhead's buttocks, who arches, cock engulfed between the girl's legs.

Clouds surge. The screen gives way under their weight and splinters into millions of needles, the images dissolve and the buildings appear again, their roofs bristling with TV aerials and chimneys, grey zinc under the grey sky. The bodies peel off in tatters, their liquefied flesh dots Jeanne's face, runs down it, and Jeanne licks, at the corners of her mouth, this rain that tastes of sex. The taste of sex, and of something else – she licks again; the liquid that soaks her tongue doesn't have the consistency of water. By the time she recognises the taste of liquid metal and carries her hand to her mouth, it is too late, the blood has invaded her lips, runs down her chin, drips onto her neck.

Looks like you just slit an animal's throat, the pharmacist remarks, hidden behind his counter, handing her a gauze swab of unreasonable proportions.

Jeanne wipes her mouth, her teeth and her reddened chin. Then she cleans the stains stuck to the counter, which the pharmacist points out to her with a rigid finger.

She scrubs zealously, but the finger constantly finds other targets, it directs her to the glassy orb of the coin tray, reveals crimson droplets hidden under the display of Ricola sweets, and despite Jeanne's diligence, and despite the time that passes, the drops seem more and more numerous. The pharmacist's finger does not weaken. It points, Jeanne scrubs, and to her it appears increasingly certain that she will remain in the whiteness of this pharmacy for eternity, occupied with erasing minuscule red stains, a torture inaugurated especially for her and carried out under the direction of that vengeful forefinger. She imagines that perhaps there will be a certain comfort in following the orders of someone else in this way.

But the forefinger relaxes; the hand suspends its course; still vigilant, it hovers circumspectly over the scene of the crime, stops, waits, then slowly folds itself away into the pocket of the white coat, where its energy wanes.

The pharmacist smiles, magnanimous.

Her body has remained opaque. They probed the heart, head, lungs and abdomen, without finding anything.

The doctor had predicted unprecedented discoveries, the high likelihood of cutting-edge operations that his very good friend and esteemed surgeon colleague – the best in Paris, a big shot, technical abilities the whole world envied him for – would have conducted with the hand of a master.

Jeanne must not give in to anxiety, she had just one thing to do: relax; science was there, gathered at her bedside. Soon, all would be clear; soon, they would know and, when they knew, they would take action. These days, there wasn't much a body could conceal from the ultra-powerful eye of medical imaging. Nuclear magnetic resonance, thermography, spectroscopy, scintigraphy, ultrasounds, radioscopy, Jeanne's body would be traversed right through. The machines would produce an immense, luminous double of her. Then, the parasitic stain would rupture the screen and the doctor, with a calm gesture, would point out the root of the sickness. There, the doctor would say, and 'there' would be defined, 'there' would be removed. Quickly, the tissue would re-construct its crystalline lattice; Jeanne's body would return to normal and allow itself, once again, to lie low.

They smeared her, palpated her, administered various fluids and inserted her into fluorescent cases where she seemed alone, but where expert eyes scrutinised what she herself would never be able to see.

She felt these looks dispersing inside her, each one patrolling the zone that the doctor had assigned it before-hand, in order that the search would not omit any hiding place. She saw herself translucent. She was afraid that her body would be coaxed into throwing open the bolts of the memory palace; terrified, she visualised the doctor's importunate wandering about, dragging his slip-on shoes and plastic hygiene cap from room to room, using a stethoscope to examine the trophies with an earnest air, surprised by strange excesses of hair growth, questioning unexpected folds of flesh, burying his nose in the embroi-dery of a testicle with the conviction of inspecting his patient's pulmonary alveoli; she was afraid of him being led to a misdiagnosis. She saw herself as a circus freak, a new species of hermaphrodite, a ready-made excuse to allow science to engage with brio in her favourite, but nevertheless guilty, activity: performance.

The Collection

The machines turned, hummed, grafted, hooted, and the body stayed silent. Nothing appeared, neither the promised gleam of enlightenment, nor her angelic double, nor the root of the sickness. There was a mumbling of hypotheses; the doctor didn't hide his disappointment.

She returns to the Hôtel Villa Lutèce. The glass front is cracked, as though a volley of stones had been thrown at it. She would like to see Room 114, but access to the hotel is restricted, the premises reserved for a Weight Watchers convention. Jeanne catches sight of the young woman in grey uniform. She is distributing name badges to the people present. With each badge she gives out, she scores through a name on a list that numbers several dozen. When she moves past the axis of fissures in the window, her silhouette trembles and deflects like a stem plunged in water.

Jeanne leaves the threshold of the hotel and follows the line of the road. She goes past the tropical pet shop, Bertrand funeral directors, a nameless garage, arrives at the pale block of a primary school, then walks alongside the endlessly dark wall of the Salpêtrière Hospital south buttress, which stretches to where the huddle of a minuscule building infringes on the landscape. After that, the road stops; after that, it's the Boulevard Auriol and its enormous towers: Chéops (35 floors, 103 metres),

Chéphren (27 floors, 84 metres) and Mykérinos (31 floors, 93 metres), three tower blocks of the Italie 13 project, three apartment buildings which were given the names of funerary complexes.

As Jeanne approaches the low house, its appearance alters. That which had seemed solid disintegrates; architectural rigour blurs into organic porosity; a state of more or less advanced decomposition animates the surfaces in a disturbing show of vitality; the facade cracks with flakes and swells with blisters; the dark blue of the drapes is dilute; lintels tilt, joints gape. It is a hotel, another one, and the opposite of the first, Hôtel Bruant – a single floor, a single star; she enters.

The five members of a family – father, mother, and their children in their thirties – all absorbed by the match playing on television, shout, The door! One of the children – a big, pale boy – gets up, sighing, and drags himself to the counter, keeping one eye glued to the green rectangle lined with white, on which red and blue particles are running back and forth. He presents Jeanne with the key for Room 3 – upstairs, second on the right – and returns to his place.

A whistle blows, close-up of a man in black, one hand in the air, brandishing a yellow card; the family members exclaim, the big boy stands up and brings his hands to his forehead, incredulous.

A falling sound in the stairwell. They freeze, the big boy hurries upstairs – he's the one in charge.

He finds the guest prostrate in the curve of the staircase, the contents of her bag strewn across the steps, her back against the wall, her head tilted. The big boy offers his help, gathers her bag, places his shoulder under the woman's to help her up. He is afraid of missing a crucial moment and, as he climbs the stairs, strains to hear the voice of the commentator and the reactions of his family to gauge the heat of the action.

They reach the first floor, the boy takes the key, opens Room 3, sits the guest on the bed, asks her if she would like a glass of water or a lump of sugar. The woman doesn't answer. Instead, she stands up, straightens her body, throws back her shoulders – she seems taller. The big boy begins his retreat, embarrassed to find himself so close to the guest now that the reasons for his presence have visibly disappeared, embarrassed above all by the proximity of the bed and by the restricted space of the room. Moreover, he thinks he hears a murmuring, the impression of suspense that precedes the possibility of a goal, he must go down as quickly as possible. But she pulls him to her, opens his black shirt with one hand and bolts the door with the other. He watches his stomach rebounding with each button that flies off.

Downstairs, there is yelling.

*

They've tried their best to call him, but he hasn't come back down, too bad for him, the play has been superb. Roberta feints past Adswenger, blind pass to Lomo, who receives, then dribbles round Hutchins, who tries to stop him, nutmegs Jawls and lets fly with his left foot, impossible curve, magic, the ball pelts right into the top corner. Gunson didn't stand a chance.

They saw the kick coming, so they yelled, they yowled, Come down!, they oohed and ahhed, they stamped their feet: they warned him. What's he up to? He's just missed the most beautiful goal of the season.

Shower stall in the corner, wallpaper and ceiling light, notice board, tourist tax, animal surcharge, YOU ARE HERE, the yells of the family rushing against the door, especially the father, who rants and raves. The big boy's hand, splayed in a star on the bed, crumples the sheet; his thin, pink nails sink into the small flowers. His breath hitches, he closes his mouth, closes his eyes, frowns. His face becomes hermetically sealed. Jeanne takes his penis in her hand and, with the tip of her tongue, circles his testicles. The big boy's penis hesitates, suspended between two states.

The slow motion replay cannot be disputed; Lomo was a metre ahead of Hutchins when Roberta passed to him. There's no arguing with that, hence the consternation. When the referee gives only three minutes of injury time, the father gathers himself, yelling, The ref's been bought! without really believing it, as a gallant last stand. The boy still hasn't come down, they pretend to have forgotten him but are no longer quite at ease, they have a limping feeling now that there are only four of them. Should someone go up to fetch him after the last whistle? Who should go? The father? The sister? Zingel approaches Gueldo's net. They tremble.

The big boy has ejaculated in her hand. She goes to rinse it in the bathroom, and hears the sound of a zip. When she returns, the boy is still there, on his feet, completely dressed, arms dangling, he obviously doesn't dare to leave without saying goodbye. Hesitantly, he whispers, Thank you, and turns the handle, but the door resists. He regards Jeanne with the air of someone tangled in a net. Suddenly it occurs to him to slide the bolt, and he hurries into the stairwell. Jeanne closes the door behind him, lies down and retrieves the simplest dildo in her collection from her bag. Through the translucent plastic, she examines the ceiling.

Flattened against the white sky of Paris, Chéops, Chéphren and Mykérinos look as though they are waiting for the riverbank district to be engulfed by an extraordinary flood, for the scaffolding supporting the overground metro to collapse, for the Boulevards Auriol, l'Hôpital and up to Saint-Marcel to freeze, for tumbleweed to blow along the deserted thoroughfares. Chéops, Chéphren and Mykérinos know that only then can they express their sublime potential. For the time being, they tolerate the folding chairs and bicycles piled up on their balconies.

While the tower blocks of Italie 13 dream of their inhuman future, Jeanne pushes through the door of the Hôtel Bruant once again. She enters into the hubbub of various matches, late lunches and ignored telephone calls – for it is never a client at the end of the line, but always an unsolicited caller, suggesting the refurbishment of the doorframes, or of the roof.

The Hôtel Bruant is bankrupt. A slow, Sunday

bankruptcy. It will soon be emptied, sold, destroyed or renovated.

In the meantime, she returns here. She likes the miniature space of the hotel, the noises that rise up to her room, the rolling of the metro and the shadow of the towers, which stretches out and covers the tiny building.

She reserves Room 3. She thought to arrive accompanied, to bring back men picked up on Boulevard Auriol, Rue Dunois or Rue Nationale, but it is with the big boy that she closets herself away. He never speaks, apart from when discomfort prompts him to utter the improbable 'Thank you' that concludes their encounters.

The family do not comment, do not blink. They stop calling to the boy when he is upstairs, they show no hostility towards Jeanne, nor any attentiveness. When she reserves her room, the employee checking her in – mother, father or child – invariably asks for her name. She spells it out slowly, they note it down with care, never anticipating a letter before she has uttered it. This tacit ritual of forgetfulness pleases her.

The boy's penis is motile. It alters when it grows erect but, above all, it looks different every time she reveals it. Sometimes round and short, sometimes long; sometimes smooth and opaque, sometimes fragile and translucent, veined with a subterranean circulation; sometimes light, sometimes heavy; sometimes trembling, sometimes subdued. The black trousers are always the same, the belt does not change, the boxers rarely.

After the big boy has gone back downstairs to rejoin his family, Jeanne stays in the bedroom and visits the room in which she has deposited his penis. She updates the memory according to the data of each new experience, with the hope of arriving eventually at a faithful portrait. But the corrections are never definitive and each new glimpse reveals the inadequacy of the memorised image.

Stretched out on the bed, lost in the detail of modifications, Jeanne sometimes falls asleep. She leaves the room two or three hours later and walks along the Boulevard Auriol, accompanied by the procession of advertising billboards, stickers and posters sloping gently towards the Seine: NATIONAL LOTTERY – LOTTO – VISA – BEEF LAMB POULTRY – MONEYGRAM – CAIXA GERAL DE DEPÓSITOS – SO-CO-SUR – SICRA – RENOVATION OF A WORKERS' HOSTEL – THAI MASSAGE – MON TO SAT – RESTAURANT COUPONS – 9:30 TO 1 – PUSH – PULL – PRIV. PARKING – PUSH – PUB. PARKING – PULL – GH PITIÉ-SALPÊTRIÈRE.

Quai de la Gare, she huddles against the damp back of a man, breathing in his scent. The man stiffens, on alert, doesn't move, waits for a sign. She could. Does nothing. She closes her eyes and goes slowly through the memory palace, whose floors feel downy. Black skin, dark veins, light, supple testicles; red hairs, glans a purplish blue as though bruised, flushed penis; penis hunched up on itself like a burrowing animal; blurred penis, tortured outline; bare cylinder, pointed-cone pediment, sex-blueprint.

Dugommier, the man leaves the train, turns back towards her before the doors close, meets her vacant gaze. A firm penis, large and focused; tight curls, nestled penis; curved line of a boomerang-shaped penis; precarious balance, dark glans; grainy skin, thickset, sullen, taking a long time to grow pliable.

At Nation, all the passengers leave the carriage. Jeanne gets off, leaving the door open behind her.

Bodies in strobe light, basslines, flashes, screams, twist-
ing, swirling fabric, flying fabric, skin, hands spread
wide, arms outstretched, dry lips and moist lips, red lips,
smudged lips, streaming eyes, glistening necks, sheen,
curves, leaps, breaths, halts, quickening, falls, whirl-
winds, ruptures, captures, skin, nails, tongue, crushed
noses, inadvertent scratches, thigh against penis, penis
against bottom, thrusting hips, rises, masses, flows,
waves, haziness, sweat, liquefactions, vibrations, puls-
ings, flares, high notes.

Red, harsh blue, floodlit, she appears,

without distinct outlines, flattened against bodies,
deliberately buried, she seizes handfuls of flesh, tries to
melt into it, a vampire through dissolution, is crushed,
smothered, hit, squeezes, licks, disappears under backs,
stomachs, hands, legs,

basslines, flashes, screams,

no more memories, no more body that belongs to
her, no more reasons or causes, in the turmoil of the

crowd she appropriates bodies, steals lives, latches on to potential stories and releases them upon the orders of the sound system, sets off again on the hunt for existences which at first resist her, but which she then penetrates with force – and there she is in the chill of an ice rink, eyes filled with the tears of a misfortune she doesn't understand; sitting at a table under a night light, writing in a language that she cannot read; at the edge of a pool, calling the name of an unknown child with all her might; in a car, deciphering a map to guide a man whose face she doesn't know. She forces access, absorbs the obscure and the unintelligible, she becomes supple again, relinquishes her smell, her gaze, her customary gestures and plunges back into the flow, holding her breath, she catches on to the trail of the life of a disappointed spouse, she follows the current, detects its twists and turns, he is a lawyer, she followed him all the way to New York, she consoles herself by keeping busy, organising outings for disadvantaged children, museums in the winter, the Bronx zoo in spring, and in summer as far as Fire Island, subway, then train, then coach and boat, deserted beach, games on the sand, going inland, Virginia stags, the giddiness of the children – excitement, hands pressed to their mouths to contain their squeals – the day slips by, the weight of the return journey descends with the evening, boat, coach, train, subway, Manhattan, Upper East Side, she opens the door to a dark apartment, the ghostly blue glow of the television spread across the walls. The rhythmic loop snaps, she switches course towards another existence flying by. There she is on the threshold of a white house, green shutters, plants struggling to grow, houses carefully aligned, somewhere like the Île de Ré, she sets a table, yellow paper napkins rolled up into tubes in each glass, counts knives and spoons, moves a plate forward, complimentary continental breakfast for one night's stay in a B&B, she stands back, admires the effect, brings a parasol closer, waits, goes back into the big kitchen, 8 o'clock, kettle, toaster, the staircase creaks, slow footsteps, another pair catches up, fast, light steps on the tiled floor, launched outside in a racket of gravel, a man and his son scatter knives, spoons, yellow napkins and glasses, the man folds down the parasol, the momentum of his movement pushes Jeanne down onto a plastic chair in the A&E waiting room at the Pitié-Salpêtrière Hospital, 3 o'clock in the morning, pain, blood pressure, temperature, symptoms, services overwhelmed, the waves of the synthesiser break against her forehead, she plunges head first, deep splashes, aftershocks, accelerando, her body loosens its ties, she dances, the undertow alternately swallows and releases her, she swims in fluorescent water, perceives only the quickening whirlpools, slips from life to life, she is that other, divorced from an ophthalmologist, alone and desperate, who searches for refuge, who hopes to meet someone serious and stable, for she is no longer that young and life is hard; she is the one who has undertaken therapeutic treatment to understand the causes of her sexual troubles and who climbs back up the knotted rope of her lineage in search of trauma; she is the hysteric, the late-night slut, the blind-drunk madwoman who allows you to strip her on the dance floor and who laughs her head off; she is the thing grounded in her complexes, who only shrugs on the skin of her body with regret when an emergency obliges her to leave the house; she is the great nymphomaniac who strives towards sublimity and cultivates her decadent image; she is the frightened one who only finds peace of mind when she is close to the bearded dragons that she watches in the vast, patiently constructed terrarium, periodically changing the vegetal decor, always adding new succulent plants, branches of polished wood, creepers, a pool with a naturalistic LED-lit mini-waterfall; a synth line rises above the crowd, stamping down the compact block of the bassline, the movements of the dancers rush to answer the call, they rise up, become syncopated, pulverising narratives into scattered snapshots. Jeanne appears, transient meteor, on both sides of the globe, no function or reason threads her from one place to the next, she is at the foot of the Cairo pyramids;

on the back seat of a taxi; halfway up a huge white staircase, her shadow concertinaed on the hard steps; bathed
in the cold light of the washing powder aisle of a Dallas
hypermarket; standing on the edge of a pavement,
waiting for the light to turn red; she dances, feels a taut
belly against her own, damp skin, a bite, a thigh squeezed
between her legs, hands, other hands, then one precise
hand which runs up the length of her back and grips the
nape of her neck, she sinks down,

White.

Silence.

The disco resumes, general hysteria, obsessive night-
club rhythms, bass drum, snare drum, shimmering
guitar, climbing brass, one voice rising higher than all
the rest, the image blurs, she loses her footing, volume
increases, blinding light, her geography destroys itself,
without halt or pause, a metro flashes from Saint-Marcel
to 25° 58' south, 32° 33' east, appears on the quayside
at Maputo, a two-toned gleam speeds flat out between
the red containers and grey silos, sowing chaos among the
dockers, who fear a collision, she dances, the freighters
slumber, the would-be amphibian hurtles towards the
channel, launches forward, takes off, carriages stretched
out in perfect alignment, suspends its flight at its apex,
she dances, the train comes to a halt between two
pointed freighters, plummets in a nosedive, a dinosaur

submerged in syrupy water, and enters the station at Bréguet-Sabin, traffic resumes after its interruption due to an individual on the tracks, the afternoon is heavy and blue, she dances, divides in two, faces her double, exchanges an enantiomorphic look, hesitates to recognise herself, the ground gives way beneath her weight, everything which could have been collapses in a fictitious roar, her heart melts in the honey of bare-stripped skin, the imprint of her venous network flashes in the search-lights, the texture of her iris defines two lips and there drowns itself, abscissas and ordinates vanished for good, she breaks apart, between the bodies, her own is just a quirk of the light – shoulders, knees, the mark of what seems to be a vulva.

Everything slows.

The music deadens,

empties the space,

shrivels away to form nothing more than a tiny square of folded paper,

the scene is paralysed along each side, figures frozen on the periphery,

the stillness spreads right to the heart of the chaos,

the outlines cease to breathe, limbs inexorably

petrified, frozen crests on a dead sea, breaths extinguish, the fixedness spreads,

time stretches out, empty.

Suddenly, the spots of colour quiver,

become denser,

reorganise themselves according to the coordinates of an invisible grid; details disappear, the picture arranges itself into squares, captures the bodies in a mosaic of cold pixels, then one of them flickers, one, two, three, a pointillist presence that detaches from the mass and, abruptly, disappears; another body follows it – one, two, three, disappears; then another – one, two, three – and then the next; bodies disappear one by one, the wasteland takes hold, then the place itself disintegrates. The promenade no longer exists, the stairs, the path and the ceiling thin out to white, the line of the horizon shrinks in one stroke, leaving just a chequered map, like the gaps left after all the faces have disappeared.

Only Jeanne remains superimposed, the single component in a shot, her position clear, she flickers, the signal weakens, vanishes.

Silence.

Black.

The club is deserted, it is 7 o'clock; they take her by the shoulders, they steer her gently towards the street, they leave her on the pavement with somnambulant murmurs. The day climbs slowly.

She crosses the city diagonally. When she reaches Boulevard Auriol, the sky has risen – rectangular and grey – the world is noisy, but the televisions at the Hôtel Bruant are switched off, the telephones silent, the curtains lowered. The low house is surrounded by a thin net. Arachnoid workers scrape at the facade and debris accumulates in big white bags.

Jeanne crosses the Boulevard the opposite way, takes the Rue Dunois, arrives at the Hôtel de l'Union. She settles in at a neighbouring cafe: she will wait for a few more hours.

In the terrarium at the tropical pet shop, the bearded dragon blinks under its blazing sun. The sandy scales pulse to the rhythm of prehistoric breathing.

The beast is listless on its bed of slate.

She slides it into her mouth.

She lets it grow heavy, take on warmth, breadth and shape, push against her palate, weigh upon her tongue.

Immobile lips, minute internal contractions: her movements have grown less frenzied.

She thinks of paper flowers that unfold when placed on water.

She moves away, and contemplates the erect penis.